Wolf on the Lake

Ed Thilenius

This book is a work of fiction. Names, characters, organizations, businesses, places, events, and incidents either are the product of the author's imagination or are used fictitiously. Any resemblance to actual persons, living or dead, events, or locales is entirely coincidental.

Editing: Durham Editing and E-books

ISBN-13: 978-0-692-35439-1

DEDICATION

This book is dedicated to my wife Debbie.

CONTENTS

FROM THE AUTHOR

Many years ago, while I was on the road as a salesman for a farm equipment manufacturing company, I actually saw a midget submarine at a local marine dealership on Highway 369. It was built from scratch for a movie prop to be sailed on Lake Lanier. It was painted a dull gray and rested on a trailer. A few months later, the submarine was reported lost due to an accidental sinking with the builder escaping and swimming to shore. The sub was later found back at the same local marine dealership, and it was on display and for sale as an oddity. The submarine was purchased by a junk dealer, who left it on its portable trailer. Within a month, the submarine and trailer were stolen. It is rumored that it sank again and sits on the bottom of Lake Sydney Lanier near Buford Dam. It is unknown if anybody died during the sinking. The cost of raising the submarine outweighed its practical salvage value. As of the date of this publication, no effort has been made to retrieve the missing submarine. As author of this book, I strongly recommend that you do not make any attempt to build your own submarine without proper permission from the United States Coast Guard, federal, and state authorities. People have died in foolish attempts to build a submarine for use in and under the water.

INTRODUCTION

Wolf on the Lake is a story about two brothers who enjoyed their summer on Lake Sidney Lanier in North Georgia. The setting could be any lake that has a dam, but this is their story. Michael graduated high school and was prepared to join the Army in the fall. Steven, who completed the eleventh grade at Hall High School, was excited about his summer adventures. Both boys continued to share their passion for history, specifically, World War II naval history. Masterly crafted and painted models of battleships and submarines lined the shelves of their parent's boat house. It is an old tin-roofed dock on the beautiful green and blue waters of Atlanta's very own water resource and recreational lake, Lake Sidney Lanier, or Lake Lanier for short.

That wonderful summer was filled with many adventures which included the brothers building a homemade two-man submarine from scrap parts. However, all of this ended when a horrific tragedy happened on the lake. A tragedy which probably ruined their chances of a future and quite possibly, their lives. For in that tragedy, a darker evil emerged to create terror and immobilize the city of Atlanta and the other states that shared this valuable water resource.

CHAPTER 1

Six Months Ago

The warm March afternoon sun had begun its business of heating up the upstairs bedroom. Spring was around the corner, and the daffodils had started to come up early that year outside the house. A few birds had settled on a power line that led to the older, red brick home.

"My father has forbidden me to see you anymore" was heard on the television as Anya and her new boyfriend Brian watched their favorite noontime soap.

Brian chuckled at the poor script and looked over to Anya for a collaborative laugh. The two sat on the edge of Anya's bed that was upstairs in her father's house. Anya did not laugh, smile, or even look up. Her long hair covered the sides of her face as she stared down at the Berber carpet.

"Anya? What's wrong?" Brian asked.

"I know how that girl feels," she said quietly.

Brian rolled his eyes in frustration as their most recent conversation was about to start all over again. He turned his body to face her. His hand reached up to touch her chin.

"What? Why do you feel this way? I have done all the things you have asked me to do. I want to prove myself to your dad. I've renounced my Christian faith, and I've studied the Quran. I can speak a little Pashto and Dari mix where I can have a conversation with an Oman. I've even grown this beard," responded Brian.

His hand pulled her chin towards him. The other hand brushed back her hair. Brian then reached to her and hugged her shoulders.

"No, Brian, stop," she replied as she pushed him away.

Brian released his embrace with her. He then stood up and straightened his white *dishdasha* robe, a garment worn by most men from the Middle East. In many countries, this robe was considered as formal dress. Brian wanted to impress her with his choice of clothing style. He wanted even more to impress her parents. Much of this was to no avail.

He looked at her. She was Persian. Her long hair was silky black like a polished onyx stone. Her body was perfumed with a honey and lavender scent. Her olive skin was soft and well cared for. Her Muslim name meant "girl with large eyes." She was indeed a princess to Brian.

He was American, born on an Air Force base in Germany to a strict military family. His father was a pilot for a B1 bomber, and his duty stations had him move his family around quite often.

Brian resented his father for having moved the family so much. He never had any real friends, and if he did manage to make a new friend, the family had to move again. He was angry at his country for ruining his life.

After his twentieth birthday, the family moved to Georgia. Six months later, a familiar large envelope was on the breakfast table. It was his father's orders with instructions to move to Italy and a follow up deployment in Afghanistan. Brian told his family he had enough. That he wanted to go to college and move out. His mother set up an apartment for him to live and for him to attend at a local community college in the area of Gainesville, Georgia, one of the thriving cities just north of Atlanta.

The family had distant relatives in Hall County that could help Brian if he needed anything. The least of anything was a place where Brian could say he had family.

On the last day before the big move, Colonel Tobias "Sabot" Brown was bedecked in his dark green Air Force flight uniform. A B-1B pilot with a large patch on his chest which illustrated a spectral-like skeleton holding a bomb. Skeletons and bones both had a unique history with bomber pilots. *Bone* was a play on words from when the first B-1 bomber was first introduced to the media back in the 80s. A reporter misread the plane's name while reading from a news monitor. The teleprompter read "B One" in phonetic spelling. The reporter accidently said "Bone," and the rest was history. Col. Brown's bomber was affectionately called *Night Rider*. He stepped out of a cab and approached his son. On the nearby sidewalk, two airmen walked by and quickly saluted the officer. He returned their salute and addressed his son.

"I know you're angry. I know you wished you had a kind of dad that stayed at home. This is what I do for a living. It pays the bills. Please don't hate your country or me. I'm proud to serve her. One day, I hope you will forgive me and try to understand," said the father softly.

Then his voice changed to one like a commander giving an order.

"Here is your Civilian Military Pass, your CMP. This card will get you on to any base, let you shop for groceries at a PX, and will even get you a free plane ride to any air base in case you want to see us in Italy or wherever we end up. You better shave off that damn *Hadji* beard and be clean cut if you ever try to use the base. Otherwise, the base guards will give you hell about the way you look," he finished.

Half angry and half heartbroken, Brian, with his head down, took the card from his father. He made a gesture to hug his dad goodbye. As he slowly approached, the father's cellphone went off. The ring tone was different: it was the *Scramble* alarm sound. His dad needed that special tone to let him know he had to rush straight to the base.

The two never hugged goodbye, and in a minute, the cab was gone, and Brian was left standing all alone once again.

CHAPTER 2

Present Day

The moon filled the night with a beautiful light on Lake Lanier; a few wispy clouds blew across from the west in the North Georgia sky. A red and white 30-foot speedboat, which had seen its better days, had just dropped anchor in Wild Man's Cove, a deep-water inlet that was ideal for any skipper wanting to take a date on a boat for some late night shenanigans. The tall pine trees that outlined the watery hide-away shielded any boat in the cove from unpredictable winds or prying eyes. Curious boaters always wondered what went on in such a location, for there always had been a tradition that if one were to get there first, no one else would anchor nearby.

"Oh, what a pretty moon," Joyce gasped.

The scantily clad blonde finished off her third glass of a cheap white wine. She wore a neon Day-Glo orange bikini which barely covered her expertly sculpted body by a talented surgeon's scalpel a few years before. Her body was a series of special surgical gifts, for she didn't have to pay for any of the procedures—not monetarily, anyway.

"Whew! This wine just went straight to my head," she mewed.

"Yeah, straight to your head and straight to my bed, my darling," whispered Carl Trip.

He was the portly captain of the 30-footer, the *Pinot Blanc.* A boat name he later regretted giving it, for a lot of his friends who knew Carl knew he had been caught peeing off the side of his boat. One night, when Carl had imbibed too many drinks, he was found standing on the boat's swim deck, naked, trying to urinate. Nothing had come out until the last second, when a small stream that could probably fill a shot glass was produced. After seeing that, Carl's friends dubbed his boat the *Pee-No-Blank*.

His cheap, red Hawaiian shirt, strained by his immense girth, adorned with many old, greasy food stains and one or more cigarette burn holes was his trademark lucky shirt. That red shirt had seen too many a night, as its wearer had tried in vain to woo too many women.

"What did you say, Carl?" asked Joyce.

As her legs and feet desperately tried to maintain their balance, the gentle bobbing of the boat made the task difficult. Like a baby fawn trying to stabilize itself just after birth, she walked aft-wards to the ship's rear cockpit, and, like a naive fawn, she stumbled into the wolf's lair.

Carl caught Joyce and eased her down to the seats to make her comfortable. She let out a silly giggle which turned into hysterical drunken laughter as she realized she had had way too much.

Thump. A soft dull sound was made along the port side waterline of the boat. Like the soft sound of a baby's plastic cup bumping against a food tray, it was a sound not meant to be heard.

"You hit the boat, stupid!" whispered a quiet voice on the other side of the cove.

Some 200 feet away from the boat, there were two high school boys crouched close to the water's edge who hoped to get very small behind a single bush.

These two shadowy figures froze motionless as they watched their remote-controlled model boat smack against the anchored 30-foot cruiser. A special gift for each of them from their uncle, spray painted with a dull-black enamel paint, the 18-inch plastic motorized boat was redesigned by them for stealth to take pictures of skinny dipping boaters. The bright moon's light barely reflected any angle or shape from the tiny craft. To an untrained eye, it looked like a black hole in the water. The tiny ship had hit the speedboat and had begun to back away in the quiet wakes that stirred around the anchored boat.

"What on earth was that?" asked the woman.

"Nothing, just some driftwood hitting the side of the boat. Come over here and sit by me; I won't bite."

The cockpit of the boat was an open area with bench-like seats outlining its perimeter. Many boaters adorned their cockpits with white or dark blue leather seat cushions. These cushions were perfect for lazy naps, rough seas, and an instant bed for dubious reasons.

"It was not my fault. The stupid antennae on our spy boat can't pick up my Bluetooth signal from this distance," Steve said.

Steve, having completed the eleventh grade at Hall High School, was wearing his favorite blue jeans and a black golf shirt that had the school's mascot embroidered on it. His older white tennis shoes were caked with the lake's mud. His brown hair was uncombed and in desperate need of his monthly haircut.

Whenever Michael got upset at his brother, he would call him out by his full first name, a mimic that he had picked up from their mother.

"Steven, I told you this would happen if you did not use the fresh batteries that Mom bought."

"She didn't get any. She told us that she was getting really tired of buying our stuff and that we should get summer jobs remember?"

Michael, the graduated senior, was also wearing blue jeans but had on a navy sport shirt that had a sailing motif. He left his boat shoes in their vehicle but wore his dad's rubber galoshes. That way he could wade into the lake and retrieve the spy boat.

"Well, let's see if the video camera feed works at this range. I want to see what they are doing on that boat," Michael responded.

Looking like a cold and calculating, long, black water spider, the little spy boat's front part was cut away to make room for a hobby video camera. Weighing no more than a half a pound, the tiny camera was nestled very nicely in the middle of the bow as to prevent the craft from being top heavy and unseaworthy. The silent craft was maneuvered again by remote control for a better view.

"Aw, baby, now come on and take off that little bikini of yours, and let's go for a swim," suggested Carl.

"No, Carl, I think that noise was a beaver, or maybe it was some kind of water creature that bumped into the boat," whispered Joyce nervously.

"I have a little friend here underneath this seat cushion for any varmints or critters."

"What's that?"

"My standard government-issued 9mm handgun. I am not supposed to take it with me when I leave work, but I figure I am an important individual on this lake. You see, I work for the Department of Natural Resources, and my job is to protect these waters from boating under the influence, people dumping their garbage into the lake, and even *a* terrorist attack when it comes to the Buford Dam."

"Are you some kind of special agent?" Joyce asked.

She began a renewed interest in her date. Her fingers slowly flowed over his red Hawaiian shirt as she began to settle down from the alarm. The woman made a teasing pull at one of the buttons on his shirt.

"Agent? Uh, yeah, I am a special kind of agent. I can't go into all the details, but I am an agent," lied Carl.

His khaki shorts rattled with loose change in his right pocket. He had already taken off his Dockside shoes and left them near the steering wheel. Carl's thick, hairy arm maneuvered around the back of his unsuspecting date.

His fingers slowly walked to the center of her back to pull open the back knot of the bikini top. His actions were thwarted by Joyce repositioning her body and giving a drunken giggle.

"Steve, he just tried to pull her top off," Michael said.

His voice rose in pitch due to the exciting view he had just witnessed with the video camera.

Michael then adjusted the zoom controls for the lens providing for a closer shot.

"Let me see," whispered back Steve.

The remote control was adjusted for a straighter view on the small viewing screen.

"It's too bad we don't have sound and color," he added.

"Well, next time, why don't we just go out and buy a high definition camera, a microphone with a boom extension, and enjoy watching our little peep shows on a 54-inch big screen television in the house? Mom will just love seeing those images in our house," Michael said sarcastically.

As the two boys totally enjoyed their new spy boat, they remained oblivious to a natural phenomenon that occurred as sound waves travel across still waters. Sound could travel an incredible distance, and with some actual clarity, along the top of the water like a skipping stone. That night, the waters slowed their swells as the day boaters called it an evening and headed back to their docks. The boys were unaware that their noisy discussion about trying to see the woman's breasts had reached the people they were trying to spy on.

"Hey, I thought I heard some people talking over there," said Joyce.

She stood up and tried to peer into the darkness from the boat's cockpit.

Carl groaned in disappointment as he stood as well and tucked in his shirt.

"No, really, I did hear something over there." She pointed in the wrong direction.

"Someone's been watching us?"

Standing up on his boat, Carl looked towards the direction that Joyce pointed while reaching for his pistol from underneath the cushion. He then began to haphazardly aim in the same direction.

"Hey! They're up. Why did they look over there?" asked Michael.

The boys watched in despair as the night of fun quickly came to an abrupt close.

Unknowingly, Michael, who still had his hands on the remote control box, accidently moved it in such a way that one of the shoulder straps connected to the box brushed up against the little boat's propeller control stick. This caused the boat to move forward. Within a span of five seconds, the little black spy boat bumped up against the back of the speedboat and made that thumping noise once again.

"What the hell?" stammered Carl.

He reached down from the swim platform on the stern to grab the little black boat. Sadly, the foolish skipper dropped his gun into the water.

"Dammit! Dammit!" screamed Carl.

He instantly realized that he was in deep trouble with his supervisor, for he had just lost his service pistol in the water. The very same pistol he was instructed to leave in his government DNR locker every evening. The clumsy skipper fished out of the water the boy's little black boat. Its tiny propellers were still turning.

"Why are you so angry, and what is that thing?" she asked.

The couple began to examine the little craft when suddenly the propeller on the black boat stopped running.

Michael and Steve viewed through the video screen in horror that their boat has been captured.

"Let's get out of here," whispered Michael.

The two took off in secret to escape detection.

"What do we do about the spy boat?" asked Steve.

"It is gone, little brother. All we can hope is that there is no way they can trace it back to us."

Both boys let out a heavy sigh as they raced out of the wooded area into a local campground parking lot. The two boys made good their escape in their SUV.

CHAPTER 3

A Wolf Emerges!

Deep in the mountains of war-torn Afghanistan, it was a cold night with a rising crescent moon. In a secured area, one of the many provinces claimed to be under the control of coalition forces, a small, dusty village named Atmuhd was nestled between several small hills. The village was finally quiet after the yearly celebration of the tribal chief's sixtieth birthday. The smell of roasted lamb and the faded campfires had begun to drift and die away.

American Army Staff Sergeant Mike Shearling was with his team of six men. Their home was a fortified outpost. Shearling looked through his night vision goggles to see the activities in the village. The fires and bright lights from some of the houses overwhelmed and obscured the filter in the vision device. He had hoped that they could have taken part in the wonderful meals the villagers had prepared. This was the villagers' night to celebrate without any foreigners or soldiers.

"Damn, that still smells good," whispered one of the other soldiers inside the bunker.

"Shoot, anything's better than your cooking or these crappy MREs we have to try to prepare and eat," replied another as he spat tobacco juice over the sandbagged wall of their temporary bunker home.

"Hey, boss, how 'bout us sneaking over the hill nearby and grab us one of the village's sheep? Johnson knows how to put it down without a noise or fuss. The villagers will think a wolf got it, and we can have us one of them good meals," asked a private.

"You dumb shit! Really? Really! The village will crap all over us for having killed some of their property. They use the sheep for money, food, and just about everything. The flock's shepherd boy would see you and sound the alarm. What would you do with him, eh? Slit his throat, too? Battalion would have my ass, and you, moron, would be shipped back stateside and court martialed," snapped Shearling.

"Yeah, if we killed one of those sheep, Pvt. Donlin here won't be able to have his prom date for next week's country club dance," smirked Johnson.

A roar of laughter erupted from the bunker as the men teased Donlin. The combat team continued through the night chuckling and kidding with each other as they tried to pass the long and boring cold night.

As the US soldiers waited through the evening, their tactical radio, about the size of a dry-cleaner's shirt box, quietly sounded as the outposts relayed status reports to each other. The radio was at its station on a makeshift table of two green boxes of ammunition and a board placed across the top. It crackled and popped quietly in the bunker as the squelch level was just barely on the static side. The peaceful silence was broken when the radio came to life with new orders.

"Charlie Oscar Papa, Charlie Oscar Papa. This is Whiskey Tango. What is your SITREP? Over," quietly squawked the battalion radio.

The situation report or SITREP was a standard query for units out in the field from their commanders. Alpha and Bravo observation posts were to the right, about two hundred and four hundred meters away respectively, while the other OPs were on the other side of the village.

"Whiskey Tango, this is Charlie Oscar Papa. SITREP normal. The village has bedded down for the night. Over," Shearling said softly into his helmet microphone as he methodically reached down to turn the radio's volume down even more.

"Charlie Oscar Papa, be advised: brigade Intel believes that you might be visited tonight by enemy militia. It seems that the tribal chief's birthday got some folks your way upset because they were not invited. Over."

Shearling's outpost looked very similar to a square, flat, and lumpy igloo as sandbags were carefully placed to form a pillbox bunker. The roof made of wood timbers and bedecked with olive, drab sandbags completed the little building as the sergeant and his men hunkered down inside.

"Roger. Understood. This is Charlie Oscar Papa. Out."

"Hadji and his brothers might be paying us a visit," said Shearling.

The squad's automatic weapon was a machinegun known as a SAW. It was brought out and other weapons were made ready. The sergeant's men knew what the intelligence report meant, and they also knew that their fun evening was over. The happy mood changed into one of sheer business in an instant.

Their bunker guarded the main entry points into the village. One hundred meters to the front lay a small foothill of some low-lying hills. It was beyond the small rise that the soldiers knew of the small flock of sheep that belonged to the village. The bunker was surrounded by a sandy and dusty kill zone of flat terrain. This allowed the combat unit to engage any enemy combatants with a full complement of weapons in any direction.

CHAPTER 4

Catch of the Night!

"Well, let's see what we have here. This is definitely not some kid's toy boat. This has some specialized paint job. That's why we couldn't see it in the water. You know what, I'll bet you we have some terrorist right here in North Georgia. Yep, they are using it to maybe spy and take pictures of Buford Dam, probably plotting to blow it up. You see this lens here on the front: that's a video camera. Hell, I don't know, but the fellows back at the lab will know how to take this thing apart," boasted Carl.

"A video camera? Hey, do you think those terrorists were watching us? Maybe videotaping me?" gulped Joyce.

"Aw, sweetheart, them terrorists saw Heaven when they spied their little beady eyes on that magnificent body of yours."

"Let's get going."

The speedboat's anchor was raised, and its motor sputtered to life as the couple headed back to the pier. The night air felt good as the boat picked up speed.

As Carl steered at the helm of the boat, he couldn't escape the thought still in the back of his mind: the loss of his gun. He could take a day or two off and pretend he was sick. This could buy him some time to look for the pistol. He knew full well he could never retrieve the gun in the deep, silt bottom of Wild Man's Cove on his own; he began to panic in secret. Anything of weight would just disappear in the muck. He also thought about a heavy duty magnet to dredge along the bottom but quickly lost that thought when he realized that the cove's lake bed was littered with several old washers and dryers that people dumped there when the lake's water level was down during the last drought. To add to his misery, the gun's primary material was molded plastic, and with a magnet swinging around on a rope in the water, the best thing he could catch would be one of those rusting hulks down below. He could use scuba gear to feel along the bottom, but he didn't know how to scuba dive.

That was when a new scheme began to play out in his head. He knew good and well that the little black boat he captured was a toy. He also knew that perhaps some kids were using it to be a peeping Tom. The make-believe terrorist theme to impress his blonde date of the evening spurred his thoughts that he could create a story just for him. This ingenious plan of his was one that might make him a hero back at work. It just might even give him the chance of celebrity status with the media. Even so much to think of the endless selfish possibilities overwhelmed him so that he flushed with an elusive smile.

I will tell my supervisor that I accidently brought the gun home after working Friday. That I discovered some secret hideout in Wild Man's Cove, and that some suspicious individuals were testing this little black boat late Saturday night. I dove into the water to catch the boat and had my gun tucked into my pants' pocket. During the swim and capture of the boat, my gun accidently fell out of my pants, Carl thought to himself.

"I don't think I feel too good," slurred Joyce.

"It's okay, babe, it was a wild night for me, too."

As if it was on cue, Joyce quietly leaned over the transom of the boat and vomited. Her dinner, the multiple glasses of white wine, even that cheesy hamburger and mushrooms she had for lunch, all went into the lake.

"That's right, babe. Feed the fishes," laughed Carl as the boat sped away into the night.

CHAPTER 5

What Do We Do Now?

The SUV climbed up the driveway as the boys made it home. The garage door opener on the visor has long been replaced by an electronic gizmo that the bright fellows had invented. Not as neat and professional as their spy boat, the garage door device had the markings of electric tape, a few paper clips, and even two AA class batteries taped to its side.

"Open the command hatch," ordered Michael.

The boys have always pretended that their home was a massive space station and that the SUV was a combat troop carrier returning from some deep space mission.

"Maneuvering thrusters engaged, Captain," answered Steve as he deftly turned the steering wheel for a perfect parking job in the crowded garage.

The boys entered the kitchen through the garage and laughed at such silly things as that moment. Yet, it was a comfort that they could use their imagination to escape the everyday routine of being home alone for most of the time. They had shown such responsibility for their young ages. Their parents trusted and respected their children's independence.

Their father was constantly on the road as a very successful and flamboyant dental cement salesman. Their mother, a talented metal sculpture artist who wielded an acetylene torch like a conductor's baton in a symphony, was constantly in demand to premiere her latest metal creation for some new avant-garde museum. The gorgeous lakeside home was a grand testament to their parents' success.

Below the house was a short and well-worn trail that led to the family's fun and relaxation spot next to the water. It was a not-so-impressive pontoon boat house. Worn-out jet skis, faded plastic kayaks, and even a beached Catamaran sailboat cluttered the lake house and shore area. This lakeside retreat was also the boy's hideout. The massive boathouse, hidden in a sheltered cove, could easily be transformed by a boy's dream. Built for the impressive home, the structure had corrugated tin sides and roof, still there thanks to a grandfather clause for older boathouses that might still retain walls to fight against the elements and protect recreational vehicles from Lake Lanier's unpredictable weather. That place was where the boys had their adventures and played.

"Now what do we do?" asked Steve.

Michael didn't answer. Instead, he started to think about their captured spy boat. There were no markings on the boat, and there was nothing on the boat to identify the owners to the authorities.

Steve, not happy to hear silence from his brother, pleaded again, "They'll get our fingerprints off the boat and arrest us!"

Michael glared at his brother and headed to his bedroom upstairs. Steve followed Michael but went into his bedroom across the hall.

Michael went into his room and sat down at his desk. The room was dark except for the desk lamp which stayed on for pretty much all of the time. A night light was on in the far corner of the bedroom between the closet and bathroom doors. His mom had plugged that little light in years ago. A bluish-green LED glow gave Michael back then a safe feeling, but now it was a beautiful reminder of his mother's love.

On top of his desk were piles of history books about the two world wars. A few strategy board games were stacked on the right hand corner of the desk. On the other end of the messy desk was a bronze, painted timber wolf in a howling pose. Flanked on each side of the ten-inch statue were two framed photos.

The first photo was of his beloved dog, Sugar, a sweet cocker spaniel that was Michael's best friend for 15 years. Sugar was always by his side. She slept at the foot of the bed next to his feet where she guarded him while he slept. When Michael was a small child, she would run to his parent's bedroom and wake them if Michael was having a bad dream or sick. When Michael hurt his knee in a bicycle accident on a broken bottle, he was confined to his bed for a week as he healed. Sugar never left his side. The previous year, Sugar went to bed one night and passed peacefully in her sleep. The picture reminded him of happier times and soothed Michael's thoughts when he was stressed.

The other picture was of Michael and Steve when they were very young. Mike, their father, built a cardboard submarine from a kit he bought at a store. The gray submarine was designed for two people. Mike built a periscope using balsa wood and mirrors. He also included inside the vehicle some wheels and levers for the boys to play with as controls. There was even a popgun like torpedo tube which shot out plastic torpedoes. The boys in the submarine dived the deepest oceans, evaded enemy destroyers and their depth charges, and sunk many enemy battleships all in the safety of the living room floor. The picture reminded Michael of his wonderful brother and his father's love in letting the brothers' imagination grow.

Michael stared at the pictures for about five minutes and then he let out a sigh and nodded his head. He stood up and walked across the hall and knocked on Steve's door.

"Come in," Steve said.

Michael opened the bedroom door and walked in to see his brother looking at his photo of the two of them in that cardboard submarine. Clearly Steve was thinking about that night's foolishness as well.

"Hey, it's cool about my boat getting caught and taken. It sucks, but I'm alright. It was a lesson we had to learn. We should've never done such a stupid thing in the first place," Michael said.

"Yeah," said Steve.

"Alright, we're done with that. Tomorrow, let's do it right. Goodnight, little brother."

Michael closed his brother's bedroom door and started to walk away. His sibling instincts made him stop and put his head to the door. He could hear Steve sniffle as if he had started to cry. Michael then realized that his actions were affecting Steve.

"I will be a better brother, buddy. I promise," Michael said as he quietly went back to his room.

CHAPTER 6

The Wolf in the Sheep

"You stupid Americans," said Abdul Mateen.

Showing complete disrespect to his new conscripts, he spat towards the group. Abdul paced back and forth considering what to do with these men. With both hands he reached up to his hair and pulled hard. Once he felt the pain of his scalp hurting, he let go and threw his hands into the air.

"You grow beards, quote a few scriptures from the Quran, speak tourist level Arabic, and you think you are all the next leaders of our movement?"

The irate leader continued to pace back and forth as he pondered the quality of the new militia sent to him to fight the coalition forces.

"I should beat you all with my shoe and call you worthless dogs than Mujahedeen," cried Abdul.

"Worthless! I am better off fighting in Syria with ISIS," he added and then said, "You betray your country and expect me to accept you all into our unit? I'll bet your ransoms are not even worth a newspaper."

Meanwhile, two meters behind Abdul, a shadowy figure watched amongst the ranks of fighters. Born in Pakistan, this victorious warrior of several battles against the Americans in the region observed in silence. His hand was scarred and was missing a right index finger. Such a scar gave testimony to the fact that he made improvised explosive devices known as IEDs. One could always tell that this type of man had a steep learning curve in learning his deadly trade with the silent reminders to prove it.

No longer accepted in open public due to his disfigurement, the quiet warrior sought solitude away from the crowds and prying eyes who would quickly alert the Americans as to his deformity that identified him as a bomb maker.

"Abdul, come here," whispered Dinesh from behind.

The two Mujahedeen warriors began to talk in secret as they observed the group. Brian began to feel uncomfortable and started to stare down at the ground as their discussion continued.

"Perhaps that one foolish American, what's his name?" asked Dinesh.

"Mohammed or Aziz—they always call themselves these names."

"Perhaps that one young American wishes to lead the assault and become a martyr? Maybe we should grant his wish. These foreign fighters will hide within the flock of sheep as they approach the village, and they will need such a foolish leader. When the Americans discover our ploy, they will open fire with their heavy weapons, slaughtering both sheep and eliminating our problem. The villagers will hate the Americans even more, and we can assault the village during the mayhem through the southern end," whispered Dinesh.

"Mohammed will lead his flock of stupid Americans and the other infidels to their deaths."

The two warriors laughed and agreed. Dinesh reached up and patted Abdul on his shoulder. The laughter quickly stopped as Abdul looked down to his shoulder and saw Dinesh's deformed hand. He broke a faint smile and gave a nod to his comrade.

The plan was simple enough, a handful of fighters would crouch and crawl their way amongst the flock of sheep; one of the Mujahedeen fighters, posing as the flock's shepherd, would direct the animals towards the village. As the flock neared one of the American outposts, the warriors would spring up from the flock and close assault the American bunker with assault rifles and grenades. If all went according to plan, the rest of the assault force would then launch an overall surprise attack on the village. Abdul would be the one to slit the young shepherd's throat in the night to retain secrecy before the fighters made their journey.

The foolish American student Mohammed, also known as Brian Tobias Brown from Georgia, would get his wish to die as a martyr that night along with the rest of the fools. The entire plan would take less than twenty minutes from start to finish and would begin at 3 a.m.

The time on everyone's watch showed 2:30 in the early hours of the morning.

CHAPTER 7

Hot Under the Collar

Brian sweated nervously through his *ghutra,* or head scarf, as he and a handful of foreign fighters waited for the signal to begin mixing into the flock. He couldn't believe that a few weeks ago he had been at home in Gainesville, Georgia.

Back then he would drive an hour south to Atlanta on a regular basis to protest the corporate greed of the United States' imperialistic behavior towards Afghanistan and other Muslim countries. He had grown bored with the anti-war rallies and the Occupy movement in and around the city.

Brian still remembered the day he met Anya Moori. She was a beautiful Arabic woman with deep green eyes that glowed the same as her passion for politics. Her hair was neatly kept under her scarf as she observed the Muslim tradition for women's clothing.

She rejected him at first. It was her father's wish not to mix religion and race. Yet Anya encouraged Brian to convert to Islam and learn the customs of her people.

"You should take up the cause and fight in Afghanistan—fight for the Strugglers," she said.

"Your Arabic is quite good and your black beard is now full, like a man's beard should be," she continued. "When you have made a name for yourself over there, you can come back to me and ask my father for my hand. He will then be proud to have a son like you, Brian."

Buoyed by Anya's challenge, a plane ride halfway across the globe and a student's visa entry later, Brian was about to fulfill his destiny for his future bride. He held his newly acquired AK-47 close to his *thobe,* a tailored, long dress shirt worn by Islamic men, so as not to betray a glint of metal within the rank and file of the sheep.

He felt a certain pride that for once his actions would have an impact. His empty life might have some meaning now. His fellow warriors were also nervous, for it seemed that the men were realizing that they were still taller, even in a crouched state, than their quiet four-legged companions.

The men calmed down when they saw Abdul had returned from the other side of the hill. He smiled confidently as he, the shepherd boy's assassin, wiped his knife clean with an old cloth. With a wink and a nod, Abdul threw the bloodstained cloth towards Brian, and Brian signaled the special party to begin their furry march into glory.

CHAPTER 8

What Can We Build Next?

Michael and Steve began the next day by hurdling down the flight of stairs to the kitchen to see what their mother was making for breakfast. The sun's rays danced and reflected off the surface of the lake. Their mother always called it her "diamonds on the lake."

"What were you boys up to last night? I heard the garage go up and then you guys slinked upstairs like something was up," asked Sonya Cotter as she prepared her boys their favorite breakfast, pancakes.

"Nothing…," was the quiet reply from Michael.

"We lost one of our remote-controlled boats in the lake," added Steve.

"I'm sorry, fellas, but your uncle gave you both a boat as a hobby for the summer. You'll need to find something else to pass the day away. Why not go to the boathouse and see if you can build something fun to sail on the lake with?" replied their mother as she stacked the last four pancakes onto the reserve plate.

The boys eagerly ate the golden pancakes on their plate as fast as they could. They both know full well that seconds could only come if their plates were empty. A game quickly started as the boys competed for the next helping of grapefruit-sized pancakes. When dibs were being called, sometimes the awful act of licking one's fingers and then touching the top pancake was the only way to keep a pesky sibling away from grabbing extra pancakes on a plate.

"Mine!" cried Steven as he claimed his third pancake from the reserve plate.

With a simple flick and a touch, his finger moved with the ease of a swordsman as he marked his prize.

"No fair," responded Michael with his mouth full as he vainly tried to gobble down his last syrupy bite from the previous victory.

"Boys, you behave. I will need my two strong men to help me check the parts and scrap iron from Mr. Maney's truck when it gets here," Sonya cautioned.

When the truck which hauled a large trailer arrived, the boys were amazed at the new materials their mother had planned for her next sculpture. Besides the normal amounts of rusted angle iron, heavy wire, and old sheet metal, the boys discovered two large residential propane tanks. These were the extra-long kind, at around 14 feet, that some home owners bought for those long winters needing heat.

The tanks were in excellent condition except both had gaping rectangular holes cut out where the old valve assembly and hinged dome used to be placed.

"Mom, why did they cut off the tops?" asked Michael.

"I needed them to be totally empty of propane, no sense in blowing us up to Heaven with a blow torch!" replied the artist as she watched her new statue torsos being carefully brought down.

"Do you need both of them?" asked Steven.

"No, just one, but they were such a great deal that I ended up buying both. You boys want to help me with that?" she asked as she reached for her flashlight and tape measure from the back of the family tool chest.

"I'll let you boys have the other one if you want to make something out of it like that army tank you always talked about. But be careful: hornets and wasps like to make their nests inside warm places," cautioned Sonya.

She then peered into the metal torso as if heeding her own words and looked for any signs of a nest. Her quick search inside the propane tank was more like an act than an actual examination.

"Mom, we're headed to the boat house," the boys responded as the two climbed onto the family's ATV four-wheeler.

"You thinking what I'm thinking?" whispered Steve.

"We can use the propane tank as the hull of that submarine we've always wanted to build. It's a perfect size for the two of us. Maybe even a third, like Jack," responded Michael.

Sonya went back into the house and began to prepare herself for a long week of welding and building. With the help of Mr. Maney and his truck, she would start on her new "David" as soon as she arrived in Savannah.

The boys rolled their newly acquired prize off the back of the trailer. Then the two used their four-wheeler as a tractor and hauled the heavy tank to the boat house. The constant rain had raised the lake another foot, but the boys knew quite well that it wouldn't last long.

"What do we do now?" said the brothers at the same time.

"Jinx!" screamed Steve, as Michael stumbled with the same challenge.

The two started to look around for parts as they took inventory of what was needed to build their new submarine.

Then a familiar scary noise rose from within the old propane tank.

"Watch out!" cried Michael.

Instantly, a reddish-brown swarm of four newly hatched wasps emerged from the dark recesses of the boy's new sub. Agitated from the dropping and dragging of the sub from the driveway down to the lake's shoreline, the wasps were looking for a fight. They hovered and darted back and forth; the winged defenders had risen up to guard their nest. Their rigid, wax-paper-like wings flittered, which mimicked their anger as they flew to their two targets.

"Let's go," Steve said.

The boys quickly ran up the trail and escaped the attack. They panted and laughed at the same time, but the boys' excitement grew quiet as the sound of a car drove up on the gravel driveway.

"It's Dad," Michael said, as they ran to their father's car.

The black, seven series BMW came to a stop. Mike Cotter, still in his business attire minus the coat and tie, put the car in park and climbed out to greet his sons. He did so with a smile, and then he secretly pointed to the shadowy figure in the back passenger seat.

"Guys… I have some sad news," said the father.

CHAPTER 9

What the…?

The sheep followed their new shepherd as Brian clutched tightly to his AK-47 under his garment. He feebly walked within the flock. The loose mob of wool and wolves rounded the protective foothill and began their last minutes, moving towards the American outpost. Several of the fighters were armed with rocket-propelled grenades, or RPGs. Quiet murmurs emanated from the flock as the fighters sounded their protest about having to crouch so painfully low.

"Silence, my brothers," whispered a fighter.

"Just a little bit further," whispered Brian to himself.

He felt the rush of adrenaline and excitement flow through his veins. He had become a true warrior for his Anya. Her father would be proud of him.

The flock continued their fatal journey towards the bunker as a cloud of dust began to rise from the march of animal and man.

At 3:10 a.m., the Americans in their bunker stirred at the commotion and dust cloud.

"Hey, boss," whispered a US soldier inside the bunker to Shearling. "The village's herd has moved. Why did the shepherd boy move them? Why so late?"

From underneath the bunker's roof, Shearling, seated on an empty ammo box, flipped his night vision goggles down from the upright position on top of his Kevlar helmet. The light magnification in the newest generation of night lenses, the AN/PVS-22, provided the US Army excellent vision for nighttime operations. As his eyes adjusted quickly to the enhanced green light vision, Shearling noticed the unusual shapes in the herd.

"What the…?" Shearling whispered.

As he squatted inside next to the bunker's sandbagged rampart, he was puzzled by the up and down shapes in the mass of animals as they approached the bunker. Shearling twisted the night lens for an even finer focus.

"Donlin, hand me my kit bag, quick," ordered Shearling.

"What you got in that bag, boss? Your fork and knife for some roasted lamb, eh?" whispered Donlin.

He handed the kit bag over amidst the nervous giggles and quieted snickers from the other occupants in the bunker. All the soldiers began to take interest in what their leader was trying to see.

Shearling reached in and pulled out a hand-sized yellow and black plastic object. With his left hand, he gently raised his Army night goggles on his helmet back into their upright position. The new device was about the size of two D-sized batteries back-to-back. Shearling turned a tiny switch on and put the device up to his right eye. Known as a FLIR, this "forward looking infrared device" was a gift from Shearling's dad. His father used the infrared heat-seeing device when he would go sailing at night and needed help when coming back to the marina. The day's heating by the sun kept the dock still warm, while the cool waters were a different shade in the sight piece. He distinguished different objects in the dark using this thermal sensor; he always managed to safely dock his boat even after several glasses of scotch and water.

"Wow. Wow. No… it can't be," Shearling said.

He quickly turned his head back to his men. The thermal sensor suddenly changed Shearling's viewpoint from eerily green sheep walking in the dark to vivid, milky white bodies and legs of the animals; the difference between the two devices was black and white so to speak. Something was askew to Shearling's observation, however: there were animal shapes walking on four legs in the herd; but there were also many two-legged animals walking in the mass as well.

"Eyes out. Weapons hot. Contact left, 75 meters out. Open up on my count of three. Here we go: one, two—"

"Wait, boss, you mean to shoot the sheep?" asked Johnson.

"No, dammit! The enemy is using the sheep as cover. Blast them before they hit us with their RPGs," snapped Shearling.

The bunker, silent and still as an old man's hat on a church coat rack, came alive with fire, tremendous thunder, bright flashes, and hot lead as the soldiers opened up with their automatic weapons. The men used everything from the unit's SAW to their own personal automatic rifles. They shot everything they had downrange. In a blink of an eye, the bunker's crew unloaded a tremendous amount of ammunition towards the herd and the enemy within its ranks.

"Cease fire! Cease fire!" Shearling yelled.

With the targets apparently destroyed, Shearling, like a football quarterback calling an audible over the gunfire, waved the back of his right hand in front of his mouth, giving the signal he was saying something important.

As the weapons went silent, the immediate sounds of steam and metal contracting in protest could be heard. The soldiers' guns had cooled rapidly from the extreme heat of the weapon's fire. The guns filled the dark night with noises that only the soldiers understood that their weapons had done their job.

Shearling picked up his FLIR again to see the results of the automatic weapons' fire. . The dead sheep and enemy combatant's bodies were still warm and displayed in his eyepiece as a mass of creamy white images.

"Shit," he said softly.

He had forgotten that body heat still remained for a while even after death. He switched back over to his night goggles on his helmet.

The green-lit vision was actually worse than Shearling imagined. In the mass of dead corpses, he could still see movement. Slain animals squirmed in pain; a hand or two of a human rose in a vain attempt to surrender. Even the village nearby that the soldiers have been protecting had started to show signs of activity. Several house lanterns were lit to see what the firefight was all about.

As the silence sank into the bunker, the squad's battalion net radio kicked in with a crackle and a bunch of static.

"Charlie Oscar Papa. What the hell is going on over there? Over," squawked the commander.

Shearling reached for the phone. He began to answer his superior's request, but in the distance was a sound of three muffled thumps from behind the hill in front of the bunker.

"Mortars! Mortars!" screamed Donlin to everyone inside the bunker.

To an infantryman, the sound of a mortar fired was unmistakable. A distant *thump* sound, similar to when someone hits a large plastic trashcan with a heavy stick, signaled to all who knew it that an explosive mortar round was on its way. Where it hit was everyone's guess, but to a trained enemy, those rounds could rain explosive death from the sky.

"I thought we greased them all, dammit!" cried one of the men inside the bunker.

"No, it seems that *Hadji* has some brothers who stayed back to watch everything from some safe spot on top of that hill," replied another.

Three large explosions tore the ground apart in the northern front of the soldiers' bunker. Shrapnel and flying rocks bit into the sandbags of the bunker as testament to the mortars' lethal effectiveness. Sand, which bled out from the damaged sandbags, reminded someone of sand falling in an hourglass.

"Shit! We're screwed. Let's get the hell out of here!" screamed Johnson.

Shearling was irritated that he had ordered his men to waste the village's sheep herd. The decision had been logical to catch the enemy before they got to the bunker and his men. He grabbed Johnson's collar tightly and shoved him back into one of the dark corners of the bunker.

Tensions quickly mounted as the men inside looked at each other as to what to do next. All were highly tense as they knew the bastards on the hill were loading a new set of mortar rounds. This time, the enemy's chances were good to hit their target with deadly probability.

Within the brief silence, the men in the bunker heard a most glorious sound from the radio. The battalion's air liaison officer announced that air support was on its way.

"Charlie Oscar Papa, I've got a deuce of heavy air support coming in on your west. We need you to assist us with the mortar locations and to illuminate your position," the officer said.

Shearling activated an infrared beacon device, similar in size to a flat silver can of sardines, and tossed it out of the bunker onto the ground. With a steady pulse of invisible light, the illuminator grenade gave the B-1 pilots the ability to see the location with their night vision goggles. With each invisible flash of the device, the bunker's silhouette looked to the pilots like a turtle on a sandy beach in their eyepieces. Attached to the forward part of each pilot's flight helmet, an optical eyepiece that looked like a kid's telescope magnifying glass contained a combined instrument with the infrared and the forward viewing camera. This gave the pilots an owl's vision of the battlefield. The B-1B bombers were on armed overwatch standby mode hovering at 22,000 feet when the liaison officer radioed for their help.

The pilots recognized the blue flashing icons on their tactical radar map as friendly forces. Special information sent by the forward controller to the pilots had the new attack coordinates and red icons representing enemy positions. The bombers quickly dove into an attack as they flew towards the outpost.

"Charlie Oscar Papa, this is Night Rider. I see your ID and will engage your enemy Tangos on the hill to your front, do you copy? Over," said one of the B-1 pilots on the radio using their special call sign, as the two wing bombers made their attack run.

"Roger that. Good copy, Night Rider. Be advised we had enemy tangos to our west below you now, 75 meters from our position," Shearling replied.

"Intermingled with the village's sheep herd. We had to—"

A tremendous explosion hit directly on their bunker's sandbag wall.

The explosion blew everybody down to the floor. A blinding flash and tremendous heat wave singed the occupant's exposed faces and burned eyebrows. The explosion sucked the very air out of the bunker and caused the American soldiers to wince in pain as their lungs screamed for oxygen. Then there was a deafening boom. A tremendous blast of noise, one that could only be compared to a lightning bolt hitting a tree right next to one's house, overwhelmed the soldier's eardrums as it washed over them. Then there was nothing. The soldier's eardrums rung, eyes blinked, and a sick feeling of nausea welled up in their stomachs. Next came tiny showers of dust, sand, and debris as it rained down on top and inside the bunker.

This time there wasn't the usual deep thump in the distance signifying a mortar round being fired. No, the sound before this explosion had a very loud whooshing hiss to it. It sounded like a big firecracker just being launched at a Fourth of July party. The soldiers inside the bunker in their stunned state knew all too well that their bunker had just gotten hit with a rocket propelled grenade known as a RPG.

"Got 'em," muttered Abdul.

The Muslim extremist threw his RPG launcher down to the ground. He reached for his AK-47 rifle strapped behind his back and signaled the last of the enemy Mujahedeen to move in from the eastern side of the bunker's position.

"Kill the survivors," Abdul said with a grizzled command.

"Up, men," Shearling coughed the order as the US soldiers in the bunker tried to recover from the blast hit.

"Charlie Oscar Papa. Charlie Oscar Papa. What is your condition?" crackled the B-1 pilot's voice from the bunker's radio.

Knocked over and covered in debris, the radio was the only thing that had not coughed or wheezed from the RPG blast.

The soldiers slowly rose to peer out from within the remains of their battered sand-bagged fort. In the choking dust inside the bunker, each man looked to the other to see if all were okay.

"Anybody hurt?" and "Who's hit?" were the questions passed around as the soldiers shook off their dazed feeling.

"Whoa! Tangos! We got Tangos to our east!" cried a soldier.

The Americans were caught off guard as a new group of enemy combatants attacked from behind.

"What the hell?" said Shearling.

Enemy rounds began to hit the bunker as the dark shadowy shapes approached over a mound. The bunker and the men inside it were in trouble.

With their heavy weapons trained for firing on the enemy in the west, the soldiers scrambled to get their firepower into position to fire back at the new enemy to the east.

The enemy's small arms' fire began to take its toll as Donlin took a hit to his Kevlar helmet and went down.

"Donlin. Donlin's down. Oh, shit.... Donlin!" screamed Johnson.

He watched his buddy fall backwards as if being hit in the helmet by a baseball bat. For a brief second, the team inside the bunker went silent. It was the first time that one of their own had been killed. That brief second seemed to last an eternity.

Footsteps could then be heard in the distance, and the US soldiers could sense the attackers had gotten closer to the bunker.

Bam, bam, bam, bam, and *bam* came the next series of explosions. The Americans inside their damaged bunker listened and looked on in astonishment at this new event. Still stunned from their loss of Donlin and still trying to fire their weapons back at the enemy, the soldiers felt a bit of relief from a familiar sound coming from above as two large bombers flew over their position.

Like avenging angels from above, the two American B-1s swooped in. Their bomb doors opened, exposing rotating racks of what looked like big green cucumbers, each about the length of a small car. The ordnance had a unique shape. Each bomb had five ribs, like banana peels, running lengthwise. Each B-1 had a wing-mounted Sniper Advanced Targeting Pod to target the enemy. The bombardier was able to precisely drop the weapons. In the air, as it fell like a graceful blossom, the outer casings fell away and released its GBU-38 bomblets onto its targets.

The bomblets looked like green, softball-sized frozen peas, each exploding and causing widespread destruction on soft targets below. Dirt, sand, and blood erupted all around the enemy attackers. The dispensing canister bombs were very effective for this kind of mission. Thrown sinew, broken pieces of weapons, and burnt clothing went into the air. The explosions decimated Abdul and his men.

In the time it took for the bombers to fly over, the attack by the enemy was stopped in its tracks as bodies exploded from the tremendous impacts of the bombs. The receivers of such firepower ceased to exist.

"That one's for you," whispered *Night Rider's* bombardier as his olive green pilot's glove touched a tri-folded American flag tucked neatly in a side pocket in the cockpit. A customary ritual that most attack pilots enjoyed, they would carry a souvenir US flag into combat, then mail the gift back home to loved ones and family members. Their flag had seen combat!

"They got them. Way to go you guys!" screamed Shearling up into the roof of the bunker as if it were the sky above.

"Charlie Oscar Papa. What is your SITREP? Over," cracked the bunker's radio again from the pilots above their heads.

Shearling and the others quickly looked over the battlefield and to each other as they came to realize they had just survived a horrific nightmare.

"We're good. Over," replied Shearling into the handheld microphone, which completely ignored radio protocol. He added, "We have one casualty, KIA. Requesting medical EVAC."

Then a long pause happened and was followed by a surprise to everyone inside.

From the dark floor of the bunker, where Donlin's body lay, a moaning sound was heard.

Barely audible from the bombers circling overhead, there was a sound and then movement which came from below.

"Hey! It's Donlin. He's alive, dammit. He's alive!" screamed Johnson as he put his hand down to touch Donlin's chest.

"Wait one. Over," Shearling said into the radio to the pilots.

Shearling, Johnson, and the others knelt down and gently raised their fallen buddy up into a sitting position. Dazed and confused, the stunned Donlin began to look at his hands. He raised his hand to touch his aching head; his fingers found the hole in his helmet where the enemy's AK-47 bullet pierced. The heavy punch of that bullet had just missed the soldier's forehead, and the force of the impact had merely knocked Donlin out cold.

"Strike that last request, Night Rider. Our casualty is good to go. You guys were angels. Thanks," said Shearling.

The B-1s gained altitude and began a new search around the mountain for more enemy combatants.

"Understood. Have a better one. Night Rider returning to station. Out," replied the command pilot as the two planes flew away.

With the sound of jet engines beginning to echo off the distant mountains, the soldiers of outpost Charlie Oscar Papa began to crawl out of their safe haven and assess the battlefield.

CHAPTER 10

A New Friend

"What's the bad news, Dad?" asked Michael. He then looked up towards his father, and his eyes passed the shoulder of his dad, glancing towards the car.

Steve was caught still looking back towards the lake where they had run away from the wasps. His mind was still in flight or fight mode because of the angry pests they had disturbed.

"Your cousin Elizabeth will have to stay with us for a while. Your uncle passed away day before yesterday," whispered the father as if trying to avoid his voice from being overheard from the quiet shadow which sat in the back.

"What about Aunt Louise?" asked Steve. "Why can't she take care of her?"

"Boys, enough! Uncle William was my brother, and you both knew he had cancer. We knew he was going to Heaven soon. Aunt Louise needs time to get herself together. Elizabeth is part of our family, and we will give her the love and support she deserves. Now be nice and behave!" snapped the boys' father as he turned and walked towards his car to open the car door.

Michael and Steve glared at each other as they followed their father to the car to see the new addition. Uncle William was the one that gave them the cool remote control speed boats, and one of which they had just lost. They thought quietly and both came to the same conclusion: she was going to ruin their fun summer.

As the rear passenger side door of the BMW sedan opened, a redheaded, freckled face teenager popped her head out from the shadows of the backseat. Quietly emerging from the car, she began looking around the property. Tall pine trees swayed as if they were welcoming her to their home in the afternoon breeze. Her green tennis shoes touched the Georgia red clay for the first time since her long drive from the North Carolina Mountains.

"How beautiful the lake is," she said softly.

Now completely out of the car, Elizabeth straightened herself up and tucked her white shirt into her blue jeans. As she pulled back her long, red hair into a ponytail, she unknowingly displayed her puffy, reddened, blue eyes from hours of crying from the loss of her father.

"Boys, this is your cousin Elizabeth. Elizabeth, this is Michael and Steven. You remember Elizabeth, fellas?" said the father.

"Sure, yeah… sure. Uh, that's right. At grandma's house in Barnesville during Wagon Days last September," replied the sons awkwardly together.

"Nice to meet you again," Elizabeth said as she held out her hand towards Steve's hand first.

Michael, obviously just as nervous as his brother, also began to come closer to his cousin. As Steve approached to shake Elizabeth's hand, his eyes grew frantically wide with fright.

"Watch out!" screamed Steve as he pushed Elizabeth back.

Michael, who knew what his brother was so alarmed about, repeated the warning and looked quickly around for the incoming threat. Their little, red-winged friends from the old propane tank had tracked them down.

To an outsider looking towards the car and family, one could see the red wasps swarming about the heads of Michael, Steve, Elizabeth, and Mr. Cotter.

The wasps flew into their intended targets like enemy dive bombers attacking trapped battleships tied to their moorings. With everyone's arms flailing like anti-aircraft guns against their attackers, the humans, overwhelmed by the assault, began to flee.

"Run!" warned the dad as he pointed towards the house. The teenagers obeyed and made for the back porch of their home.

Elizabeth, stunned and amazed by this odd welcome, was the first to feel a wasp's sting. Her right forearm suddenly jerked in response as intense pain from the stinger began to register. The pain receptors in her skin began to sense damage and alarm as the poison began to spread. To Elizabeth, it felt like hot candle wax spreading slowly across her arm. The peripheral nerves in her fair skin sent chemical signals to her brain as to the danger. The message, travelling faster than a bolt of lightning, reached her brain with such speed that an imaginary "pop" or "bang" sound could be sensed in her head.

"Owww, shit, go away!" screamed Elizabeth as she followed the others to safety.

In a matter of seconds, the attack was over. The wasps retreated back to their lair, satisfied that they had done their worst.

The group panted and huffed for breath on the porch in the humid air around the lake. Everyone began to look at themselves to see if they had any of their little attackers still clinging to their clothes.

"Are you okay?" asked the father as he checked over Elizabeth.

He then looked at the reddened bump on her arm that was beginning to swell.

"I'm okay," she said embarrassingly. "I am so sorry for saying a cuss word, but y'all have some mean wasps done here on the lake."

At that moment, they all laughed. Adrenaline and exhaustion filled their veins as they all realized that this unintentional surprise was needed to help break the ice and had instantly formed a new friendship.

With a few pats on her back, the brothers welcomed their new friend, and everyone walked from the screen porch into the kitchen.

CHAPTER 11

What Do We Have Here?

The bunker team of Charlie Oscar Papa began their search of the perimeter and surroundings. The enemy attack seemed to them to be over after the bombers' attack. Shearling took half of the team and the unit's medic to the dead pile of sheep and enemy fighters. With guns drawn, the men were not going to be surprised again by any tricks. The gruesome mass of bodies of both man and beast overwhelmed even the seasoned American soldiers to view.

A few sad bleats from two sheep that had escaped the wrath of the bunker's defensive firepower sounded from the other side of the pile. Shearling raised a gloved hand and made a fist in the air. The signal to stop and pay attention was quickly observed as the men paused to listen and watch their commander's next order.

Silently, Shearling raised his right arm which held his automatic rifle and pointed to one odd-looking group of dead fighters. A noise similar to a moan emanated from beneath the dead bodies. The combat group crept forward with their weapons at the ready. Private Donlin moved ahead of Shearling and pulled on the lifeless arm of one of the dead fighters. As he did so, the dead fighter slid off the top of the subject that had made the noise.

"What do we have here?" asked Donlin.

"Oh," moaned the mangled fighter as he fought back the pain in his thigh from being nearby a blast hit from a grenade during the firefight.

Shearling and his men readied themselves as to this new threat. Since most Mujahedeen fighters would not surrender, there was a good chance that a grenade with the pin pulled was hidden somewhere. The captured hoped that this final act would deal death and that the explosion would kill just one more enemy soldier.

"Stay down and don't you move an inch, you mother, or I'll blow your ass to smithereens!" screamed Donlin.

He pointed his rifle to the back of the wounded fighter's head. The unit's tension got ratcheted up another notch with Donlin's stern warning. There was a moment of silence as both sides tried to figure out what was to happen next.

"Donlin, you dumb ass, the guy doesn't even know what you said. You were supposed to say *kefeyay!*" shouted someone from the group.

Imitating hands raised in the air, Donlin gestured to the enemy fighter to do the same. He added a belated, *"Kefeyay!"*

Shearling waved his hand in protest to his men and ordered the insurgent to be searched carefully. They kept the wounded man still; Donlin and a few others checked the individual and also dusted him off. The medic approached and did a quick look over as to what his injuries were. He saw nothing wrong with the prisoner, and the medic stood up and approached Shearling.

"All he's got is some bruising and maybe his ears are still ringing a bit from the blast. Other than that, I'd say he got knocked cold and woke up only to find us holding him prisoner, boss," reported the medic.

"All right. Pick up that piece of shit, and let's bring him back to the bunker," grunted Shearling.

Just as Shearling's men bent over and started to pull on the prisoner's arm to pick him up, the prisoner astonished everyone present.

"I'm an American," complained the prisoner.

"What the hell did you just say?" asked Donlin.

"I am an American citizen. I was being held captive by these barbarians, and they forced me at gunpoint to help attack your base with these other fighters. I am just a student at the local university. My parents offered a reward for my release, but these men just kept the money," sniffled Brian.

"I was on my way to this village to teach the young children math when they captured me. Please help me get home. I live in Georgia, near Atlanta," Brian added as he faked a few tears and a wimpy cough.

Stunned by this confession and surprised by their capture, the Americans were left dumbfounded. The confusion lasted for a few seconds until Johnson, who was carrying the unit's portable radio on his back, stepped up and asked Shearling a question.

"Boss, should we call this in? Plus we can do a hand swipe to see if this guy is a bullshitter," Johnson whispered.

Shearling acknowledged and reached into his pack and pulled out a black electronic box about the size of a shoebox. It had an attached plastic zip lock bag. Opening the plastic sandwich bag, he produced a wrapped towelette. Next, he unwrapped the small, white alcohol pad and turned on the electronic box. This handheld box, seen in every major US airport, was used by the TSA to check a suspect's finger or hand to pick up traces of gunpowder or plastic explosive residue. If there were some, then this fellow had fired his AK-47 or handled an IED.

"Hold out your hands," ordered Shearling, and he swiped Brian's hands and fingers with the cloth.

Satisfied that he had wiped any of the logical places where residue would linger, Shearling put the swipe cloth into the receiving end of sensor. It took only a few seconds for the results.

"Nothing," Shearling and Johnson said softly at the same time.

Brian then realized that either the sensor was broken, these men did not know what they were doing, or tonight was his lucky night. A small but barely noticeable smirk broke out across his lips.

"You see, I am an innocent prisoner of these men. I would never harm my country or you, and they made me do it," Brian said in defiance.

"Check his weapon," Shearling ordered.

Donlin picked up the dirty assault rifle that Brian had carried and pulled back the chamber to check for a round. All he found was a sand-filled and rusty old AK-47 that had not been fired in several years. The gun was empty.

They gave me a broken rifle? I was a warrior, ready to fight and die for my religion, my beliefs, and for my Anya, Brian thought to himself. Feeling rejected and made a fool of by his Mujahedeen brothers, he held his head down in shame.

"Boss, battalion wants this asshole delivered back to the embassy. Seems like they know of a student kidnapped and some form of ransom paid and that this might be him," cried Johnson as he began to fold up the radio's whip antenna back into its rolled up shape.

Stupid idiots. They think that student is me, fine. I am going home. Maybe Anya will think of me as a hero now, Brian thought to himself, and then added, *I will fight again. Long live the Strugglers."*

"I am going home to Georgia, yes?"

"Yes, you lucky dumb ass, you are going home to see your mommy and daddy. Do us a favor, kid, don't come back. You might not be so lucky next time," said Donlin.

The soldier then pointed a finger to Brian's head as he made a gesture like an imaginary pistol shooting the young student's temple off.

CHAPTER 12

Lost and Found

The black DNR truck rounded the corner of the back entrance to the regional office of the Department of Natural Resources which oversaw Lake Sidney Lanier. Carl had nervously planned out how to tell his lie and how he lost his service pistol in the lake when he was out last night on the boat. Dressed in his DNR uniform which desperately needed dry cleaning, Carl did not realize that he had accidently buttoned his uniform shirt in the wrong sequence. A quick look in the rearview mirror confirmed Carl's suspicion that he had sweated profusely over his face and neck.

Carl drove to a parking spot underneath the two pine trees that offered shade to the building. He went over his imaginary story one more time in his head. He had to, for losing one's sidearm was a terminating offense and could come with a stiff fine as well. Convinced that he had an excellent excuse, he winked at himself in the truck's mirror and proceeded to the office. As he approached the side entrance door, he saw his reflection in the door's glass panel. The reflection highlighted Carl's shirt and the poor job he had done of dressing himself. Now embarrassed and disheveled, he quickly walked to the bushes that adorned the backside of the building to redo his buttons.

While Carl experienced his wardrobe malfunction, the side door opened and out stepped another officer. Bill Gillette was a senior officer and the second in command at this station. This gentleman was clearly upset; he quietly grumbled to himself. Bill lit a cigarette and puffed deeply as if to make his problems go away. Since this wasn't the smoking area, he discreetly looked back and forth to check if anybody was watching. His strategy worked until he heard a noise from the shrubbery behind the building. He flicked away his cigarette, and he peeked around the corner.

"Carl? Is that you? What the hell are you doing, son?" asked Bill.

With his pants unzipped, Carl fumbled his way into shoving his t-shirt and green dress shirt into his pants followed by a quick zip-up. His face was a bright red, like that Hawaiian shirt he wore on the previous night's date.

"Uh… uh… yes, sir. I wanted to look sharp today, sir, and noticed I wasn't ready," replied Carl.

"You look like some child predator waiting in the bushes, you moron. Get yourself together and see me in my office. We have got a serious problem about something missing from the weapons locker," Bill said coldly.

With that statement, Bill turned smartly and proceeded back to the side door entrance and disappeared.

"Shit," whispered Carl.

His scheme melted away now that Bill knew his pistol was missing. Images of being fired began to creep into Carl's mind. With everything finally tucked away, Carl began his slow walk to Gillette's office.

"Alright, Carl, where's the pistol? You better tell it to me straight, or I will personally drop kick your butt out to the curb! You get me?" Bill screamed.

A few seconds passed, which seemed like hours to Carl, before he replied. Carl had no other story to tell, so he trusted in his original plan and began to spell out the strange details.

"You see, sir, last night I followed up on this internet date with this gorgeous chick. She was all over me because I have my boat. I wanted to impress her that I carried a gun and a badge and, well, it worked. I mean, it worked until I caught some kind of spy boat," Carl droned on.

"Spy boat?" Bill asked.

"Yeah, I got it in the back of the truck, sir."

"So where's the gun?" snapped back Bill.

"It fell out of my pants pocket as I leaned over the rail to pick up the little boat. It fell out and dropped into the lake in Wild Man's Cove. I wanted to use a powerful magnet on a line to fish it out, but that cove is covered in old washing machines, refrigerators, and all kinds of junk on the muddy bottom. The spy boat could be part of some terror plot to blow up the dam," Carl said as he prayed for some miracle.

"What the—" Bill had to cut his sentence short as a secretary walked passed his office door.

"You stupid idiot! I have to write this up, upstairs is going to fire your ass, and I am going to be out of an officer with Labor Day coming up!" cried Bill.

"Wait, sir, I got a plan. Let me stay on, serve during the holiday without my pistol—or I could use Halloway's gun. I can find out more about this spy boat—be a hero. And the bosses upstairs won't mind that your team stopped a terror plot," pleaded Carl.

Bill paused for a moment. He knew full well that Carl had lied through his teeth. However, the terror plot had always been in everyone's mind back in Washington. All the top brass had planned that the bridges, dams, and malls could be targets for attack by suicidal maniacs. The Labor Day holiday would be a great opportunity to inflict a lot of damage and carnage. The wonderful prospect of a discovered terror plot before the holiday might give Bill the big push he needed to get to the top. With enough publicity and a little bit of showmanship, it could work. Of course, if it didn't, he could still fire Carl anytime he wanted to cover things up.

"Okay, Carl. This better be good. Show me the spy boat."

CHAPTER 13

A Time to Think

A couple of days had passed, and the boys with Elizabeth head back down to the boat house to start work on their submarine. With her can of wasp spray, Elizabeth was prepared for the worst.

"Where's the nest?" she asked.

"Somewhere inside the sub. Better just spray both front and back, just to be sure," said Steve.

Elizabeth shook the can a few times and sprayed the insecticide as suggested by her cousin. Fearing some form of reprisal, she jumped back after the spraying. With no response from the old, silver propane hulk's defenders, she felt a sense of satisfaction that she had paid back some vengeance.

"Hey, not so much. We are going to be inside that thing when finished, and I don't want to smell the fumes," fussed Michael.

"What? Are you really making a sub to ride around in? How cool is that," she replied.

Michael and Steve continued their assessment and started to scavenge around for parts to build with. Angle iron, steel pipes, and other materials were abundant near the boat house, as their artistic mother piled many of her scrapped sculpture materials there.

The newly acquired propane tank rested askew, leaning heavily to the right in the sand and pebble rock shore of the lake. The jagged edges of the cut-out top on the tank were not as bad as one would think. Probably cut by a welder who wanted to save the upper portion for some other use, the propane tank was going to make a fine hull for their submarine. Two lift hooks, each shaped like a child's musical triangle, were on opposite ends for lifting. Propane suppliers usually used a crane to pick up the tank and place it on the customer's concrete pedestal. Crude metal feet on the bottom of the tank looked more like metal cheese wedges than bases.

As he tossed down another pile of scrap iron, Steve asked, "Okay, Michael, how are we going to make the sub move?"

"Well, I thought an electric motor—just like our spy boat you lost," answered Michael sharply.

"The batteries can be placed on the floor long ways, linked together and covered by some planks that we can sit on. The motor would be Dad's big industrial electric motor that's on the pontoon boat. You know, the one he uses to move around with," he added.

"Won't he miss his stuff, guys?" asked Elizabeth.

"Nope. Dad hasn't been down here in a long while—since your dad got sick. He still has that pontoon boat just like your dad's boat. It's over there," Michael said softly.

He nodded in the direction of the boat house.

Elizabeth took her cue and walked over to the shed on the water. As she entered, she immediately felt a sense of sorrow and of wonderment as she viewed their pontoon watercraft.

"It looks just like ours," she said through the doorway.

"Does it run?" she asked as she spun around and climbed aboard.

"Hey, Elizabeth, don't get on. Aww… it won't run. We tried already, several times," pleaded Steve.

As the boathouse door slowly began to close, the two boys stood and started in unison walking to the boat. They could hear Elizabeth as she fumbled and clambered about on the boat's deck and engine compartment.

"Found them," she said like a kid on an Easter egg hunt.

She smiled as she held up the boat's spare engine keys. Then she knelt near the back of the boat close to where the engine was bolted to the transom. The flat panel was the back part of a massive skeletal frame that held the boat and the two pontoons together. While there, the boys saw her reach over and move a lever on the engine. She then proceeded to the gas tank and squeezed three times on a black, ball-like device that acted as a syphon, bringing in new fuel to the engine. Like on a quest or a lab rat in a maze, Elizabeth went back to the engine and pulled on a throttle then back to the fuel tank and repeated this process twice. The boys stared in bewilderment as Elizabeth conducted her moves on the boat deck.

"Here we go!" she shouted.

With a turn of the boat's key, a warning alarm sounded, dashboard lights flickered, and the engine sputtered. The noise continued until the motor sprang to life. With a ton of white smoke and a horrible roar, the engine started to run and churn the water.

Amazed, the boys entered the boat house and quickly climbed on board.

"How did you do that?" Michael asked as Steve nodded in approval.

"This boat hasn't run in a year and a half. We never could get her to turn over. She always would crank, but she never turned over," Steve commented.

"You have to turn on the gas valve on the engine. Y'all never did that, I'll bet cha," Elizabeth said laughingly. She added, "Come on, let's get some fresh gas and take this old gal out for a spin."

"No, turn her off. We'll have fun later, and, besides, we have not checked for wasps on the boat," Michael said.

He then reached over and turned off the engine with the key on the dashboard.

"Or snakes," Steve added.

"Yikes! I'm out of here," Elizabeth laughed as they all scampered off the boat.

CHAPTER 14

Briefing and Donuts

The coffee maker had finished releasing its last drops of black morning goodness into the glass carafe. A box of donuts was quickly rounded up, and the piece of tape on the package was pulled away. A dozen glazed donuts were suddenly exposed. The room's occupants began to move in a catlike prowl towards this wounded prey of yeast and sugar. In the center of the room was a display of charts and books and the little black boat on the conference table. Bill, Carl, and the other officers gathered round and prepared themselves for the security meeting. The toy boat had been carefully dissected and remnants of fingerprint dust remained on the black hull and keel. The boat's small video camera and its wires—even the electric motor and batteries—were carefully displayed on the table.

Chairs began to be pulled back, and the officers found their places. A flat screen monitor blinked to life on the wall at the end of the room. As the demonstration was being prepared by Bill and Carl, a sense of trepidation clung in the air around the men.

"Gentlemen. Carl, here, discovered what perhaps might be a precursor to a terrorist plot to attack the dam. This reconnaissance probe had a very sophisticated video feed to an operator who had a viewer and controls to steer the boat. This paint job on the boat is from a model maker's spray gun. The enamel paint was a flat black so as to be virtually invisible at night; the fingerprints lifted have no hits on our database computer. Chances are good that these are new recruits just off the boat," Bill said in an official tone.

The room went silent. Coffee cups were quietly put down. The last bite of a donut was swallowed as the men pondered and strained to comprehend that terrorism could be in their area.

"The Corps of Engineers needs to be advised of this finding," said an agent from the table.

"No, I don't want this to get out yet," answered Carl as he sheepishly looked back at Bill.

"Carl's right. The Corps does not need to know anything until we have enough information. Plus, those idiots would talk to the press or something," snapped Bill.

The men chuckled and looked at each other as Carl and Bill continued with the briefing.

"Carl picked up the boat from the water as it was cruising around his motorboat the other night near the dam," continued Bill.

"It is my belief that this is a serious threat, and that this calls for us to begin Operation No Chastise. And we start today," Bill said with a serious tone.

"Captain Gillette? Really? This is absurd. Carl finds a toy boat, and we are all supposed to be on high alert to think it's a major attack on the dam," said one officer.

Another officer, wearing a green rain jacket, threw a pencil onto a legal pad that he was using to scribble on.

"Shut your hole!" Bill barked.

"Sir, with all due respect, may I please speak freely?" asked an officer.

Bill gave a slow nod and crossed his arms while standing behind the lectern. Carl's face began to turn red as he reached over and grabbed his third donut from the box, glazed sugar stains already evident on his pants' right pocket.

The responding officer continued his protest, this time with a more tactful approach.

"Sir, everyone has heard a rumor that Carl has lost his firearm, and he used this boat thing to make you think this is a terror weapon. He just wants to avoid getting into trouble," he said.

"No," Carl tried to scream yet choked in protest as parts of a donut spewed from his stuffed mouth onto the conference table.

The men dodged the grisly projectiles of food as they moved from side to side.

"The gun locker has eight slots for our pistols. Sgt. Peters is out on patrol with his pistol, and everyone else is here at this meeting. All of us have to turn in our weapons as we enter the command post. There are only six guns in their cubby holes. So who is packing?" the officer with the jacket continued.

The other men in the room started looking at each other to see who still had his sidearm in his holster. All were empty, and Carl began to sweat.

"Okay, fine. So Carl has lost his firearm, and he will be put on administrative leave. I still insist that we are under the beginning of an attack, and we will begin Operation Chastise. Am I very clear on this?" Bill sternly ordered.

The room filled with a heavy sigh as the men nodded in agreement to their new assignment. Chairs began to be moved back from the table as the men stood. The now empty box of donuts was tossed into the trash can near the conference room sink. Someone filled his big, plastic coffee mug before he left the meeting. Carl was evidently angry as he stared at the accusing officer.

"You son of a bitch. You just had to be the good little officer, you piece of—" Carl was cut off.

"Carl! Enough. He's right," Bill said.

It was clear that Carl was caught in the act of trying to play Captain Gillette. However, his use of the toy boat did start into motion a carefully constructed plan to begin a special observation and surveillance of the dam and its surrounding property.

The team went their separate ways while Carl followed Bill back to his office.

"Well, buddy, I tried to help you, and you helped me with this evidence and on getting the men focused on this assignment. Now, I have to let you go on leave for three weeks without pay. I could've fired you, but I like you, Carl, and you deserve this break. Now grab your gear, sign this discipline form, and come back ready to work at the end of the month," Bill said.

He patted Carl on his back like a football coach telling his field goal kicker that it was okay that the missed field goal caused the team to lose the game.

In a matter of minutes, Carl, with his personal gear, was in his assigned DNR truck that he was allowed to continue to use and was driving out of the parking lot.

"They'll be sorry," Carl said.

A strange glaze washed over his face. As his embarrassment turned to anger, so had the color of Carl's face turned from red to ashen.

CHAPTER 15

A Free Ride Home!

Brian found himself being shuttled around like an unwanted Christmas gift. From Humvee, to transport helicopter, back to a Humvee, Brian with his escorts made their way slowly to the capital, Kabul. The small convoy of three Humvees carried Brian, a small detachment of eight Marines, and an embassy officer who acted as a liaison.

"I've only had this position for the two months since I got out of college. You are my very first real assignment," shouted the young embassy liaison inside the Humvee.

Brian glanced over to him and produced a small smile. Then he looked outside through his side window as if searching for some answer to his predicament.

The Humvees entered the outskirts of the city. It had begun to be another dusty day for the citizens of Afghanistan's capital as the winds swept in from the west. The silence in the vehicle was uncomfortable. The soldiers despised their human cargo, and Brian, who hated the thought of being nothing more than a piece of fruitcake that nobody wanted, sat emotionless.

"Almost there," shouted the Marine driver towards the back of the vehicle.

He was not really trying to break the tension, but he wanted everyone to be on alert as the convoy was nearing its destination.

Going through a pair of buildings, the convoy slowed to a four-way stop. The heavily armored, four-wheel vehicles were several generations more advanced than their predecessors, featuring bulletproof windshields and windows and extra armor plating attached to the floor, sides, and roof.

The Humvee had regained some of its versatile appeal from once being the unfortunate, after-the-fact IED finder.

"Boss," said the driver as he noticed several men gathering on the far right hand corner of an abandoned building.

"They don't look too happy to see us," whispered another Marine in the vehicle.

"You guys seeing what I'm seeing?" squawked the Humvee's radio as the rear Humvee was slowing down from behind.

"But we're in the city. This can't be. The embassy's secondary office is just around the block. Hurry," said the embassy official.

"Warm it up. Get hot!" shouted the convoy commander to his men while at the same time he answered the radio call from the rear vehicle.

As if on cue, all three Humvees opened their top hatches. The .50 caliber machine gun crews popped out and readied their weapons. The Marines inside readied their automatic weapons, and Brian began to tense up.

The commander, Lt. K. Woods, a lanky, crew-cut Texan from Laredo, reached into his mouth and pulled out a dark brown wad of chewing tobacco that he had held in his cheek for far too long. Spitting the leftover remains of the tobacco juice onto the floor of the Humvee, he changed the vehicle's second radio frequency to the command net that acted as an overall station channel for the embassy's immediate defense network.

"This is Hotel Six calling Hotel Eight. Hotel Six calling Hotel Eight. Over," Woods said.

The boys in the back started to chuckle. Using the code name for the smaller embassy annex as a well-known hotel chain always sounded funny. This building, attached to a heavily guarded runway used by the military, was used for assisting in the transportation of diplomats, dignitaries, and other personnel back to the States or to other destinations.

"Hotel Six, this Hotel Eight. We read you. Are you close by?" asked an individual on the other end.

"Roger that Hotel Eight. Be advised we have a suspect welcome committee of four Tangos on the corner of—"

An RPG explosion cut off the last transmission of the commander as the convoy found itself in an urban ambush.

"Holy shit!" cried a Marine inside the lead Humvee.

The dazed men inside shrugged off the stun effects of the grenade's blast. The RPG had missed and had exploded directly between two vehicles. The gunners, manning the 50s on the Humvees quickly ducked below for protection inside their four-wheeled fortresses.

"We're under attack! I say again: we are under attack!" screamed Woods into the radio.

Forgetting radio protocol, he quickly identified that he had four enemy combatants to his front and perhaps one or two with an RPG off to his right behind one of the buildings.

Both guard Humvees opened up their doors and spilled out Marines who quickly formed a defensive perimeter around their damaged vehicles. The machine gunners sprang back up from within and began shooting back at the attackers.

"Why are you so important?" asked the embassy official, who was by now crying with fear, to Brian.

Brian, also extremely fearful, could only shrug his shoulders as he looked out of the rear passenger door window.

The fighting intensified as bullets and shouts of orders bounced off the walls of the two buildings. Both sides were quietly amazed that no one had been killed or injured by the first assault. The four combatants, shooting their AK-47s wildly, quickly scrambled for cover as the Marines' .50 caliber rounds began to pepper the walls of the buildings on the opposite side of the intersection.

Sirens could now be heard in the distance as a QRF, or quick reaction force, was racing towards the sounds of the intense fighting. To the side of the stopped convoy and down an alley, enemy activity and some commotion could barely be seen in a small cloud of dust.

"You missed," said one of the two men who had fired the RPG rocket.

"You try and fire that damn thing," replied the other.

"It kicks like my uncle's donkey. Here," he said as he handed the still-hot rocket launcher over to his younger companion.

An unusual sight, the two militia men, well-dressed as Arab businessmen in their white *thobes* and red, checkered head scarves also known as *kuffiyehs,* tried to reload their older model RPG launcher with another rocket grenade. American bullet rounds were beginning to ricochet closer as the two men frantically tried to reload.

"Okay, it's loaded. Now kill them," the older one said.

The two men maneuvered around the corner of the building to get a straight and clear shot at the side of the American Humvee in view. Like two mischievous school boys playing with a lit firecracker, they scrambled to ready their shot. Fear, excitement, and anticipation swept over them as they nervously aimed the shoulder-fired weapon.

"Here it goes," whispered the younger street fighter as he squeezed the firing trigger on the RPG.

"No, wait!" cried the other.

He tried to push the back of the rocket launcher away, but it was too late. The rocket's motor ignited and let loose a tremendous boom, flash, flame, and smoke from the exhaust end of the RPG launcher. Little did the man up front realize that his compatriot was standing too close behind him when the rocket launched. The recipient of the rocket blast was pulverized into a mass of bloody pulp. His proud clothing was then a bloodstained pile of cloth. The shock waves of the fired rocket had ripped through his body, broken his rib cage, and collapsed his lungs, which killed him instantly.

The warhead of the RPG flew to the left and skimmed along the building's wall as it harmlessly passed the targeted Humvee. It exploded on the far side of the street which destroyed a front door to a small business that had prayer rugs on display in its windows. Broken glass and fragments of the old door were thrown into the street as the explosion completed its cycle.

Stunned by his foolish mistake, the man who held the RPG launcher threw down the used weapon and quickly knelt down to hold his friend in grief.

"Over there! Shoot!" shouted a Marine to his fellow turret gunner.

From the lucky Humvee, the gunner toggled an electric switch at his waist inside the vehicle, turning the armored turret gun towards the RPG team. A faint whir sounded as the gears traversed the 90-degree facing with electronic efficiency but was quickly silenced by the deafening roar of its .50 caliber machine gun. The American weapon opened up on the man who knelt beside his dead comrade. The Humvee shook in rhythm as the heavy gun fired seven rounds within three seconds.

The armor-piercing rounds from the Marine's heavy machine gun were designed to destroy light vehicles or even open up a brick wall with ease. However, since the target for this gun was made of flesh and blood, the bullets hit with such velocity and impact that any living creature would simply break apart piece by piece. In a spray of blood and sinew, the body parts exploded: first an arm, then a shoulder, then a head. Within the three seconds, those two men were gone.

The forward Humvee continued its assault with its .50 caliber. The heavy rounds from the turret-mounted machine gun caught two of the four assailants across the street before they could effectively escape. Their bodies met the same fate as the RPG team in the alley. The battle was over that quickly.

Lt. Woods looked over his men both inside the vehicles and outside as he assessed the damage. He accounted for all of his Marines. He quickly glanced into the vehicle that held Brian and the embassy official, and to his horror, he saw an awful site.

"Shit!" he yelled.

Inside the Humvee, the embassy official was slumped over. The Lt. reached up and touched the official's neck with two fingers. Woods tried to feel for a pulse; his hand then touched a gooey spot. He recoiled quickly; his fingers were covered in blood as the body of the embassy official fell forward. Brian sat on the other side of the Humvee and was aghast with fear. It seemed that during the brief melee, a stray enemy round had ricocheted from the street into the vehicle and found its last stop.

"He, he… just fell over," stammered Brian as he realized he could have easily been hit had he sat in that spot.

Woods paused for a second, and then he returned to the official's slumped body. He thought he had heard a gurgle or a slurred word come from the official's mouth.

"Get... him… on the… plane…," whispered the official as the last of his breath left his body.

His left hand, clutching a manila folder filled with documents and a picture of a young male college student, slowly let go, and the folder slipped free to the floor of the Humvee.

Woods paused for a few seconds out of respect. He then pulled back out of the Humvee to begin barking new instructions to his men.

"Mount up. We are getting the hell out of here. The embassy guy bought it," said the lieutenant.

He looked around once more; then he radioed the embassy.

"Hotel Eight. Hotel Eight. This is Hotel Six. We have engaged six enemy Tangos on foot: four KIA; two, whereabouts unknown, estimating they are headed east. We have one friendly KIA with no wounded, and we are egressing to the runway. Please have the bird ready for evac. Over," he said.

While the troops around the Humvees hurriedly began to obey their commander's orders, Brian looked down to see the folder that the embassy official had dropped. Stealthily, he picked up the folder and opened it and found, in plain language, information pertaining to the missing college student. He memorized the student's name and hometown on the biographical data. Eerily, he was amused how the picture looked similar to him but wasn't the same.

"Yeah, sort of," he said quietly, sure he could imitate this person and get back to the States.

As he flipped through the documents, Brian read where the student's parents were meeting the military transport when it arrived in Atlanta where they would pick him up at Dobbins Reserve AFB. A simple reception would greet the plane, and, per the parent's request, no news reporters would be present.

Wait. Needs one touch up, Brian thought to himself as he quietly reached over and, with one finger, dabbed into the embassy official's bloody neck to get a drop of drying blood.

"There," he whispered.

Brian made some faint smears with the blood over the copy of the student's passport picture and wiped the rest on the other papers. One could still see a young man in the picture, but the blood stains blurred the image and made the documents undesirable to be read thoroughly or even held.

Brian quickly closed up the folder and held the paperwork in his lap. As the soldiers began to climb back into the vehicles, Brian handed the documents over to the Marine lieutenant respectfully as the soldier climbed into the front seat. A Marine adjusted the shoulder harness in the Humvee's backseat to hold the dead official firmly in place as the convoy motored ahead.

In four minutes, the convoy arrived at the fortified gates of the runway. The guards quickly motioned the convoy through as other guards watched for any additional attacks. The three Humvees continued on and made it to the Air Force C-5M Galaxy. A large military cargo plane, the rear ramp was open on the plane for easier entry. The noise from the four jet engines that ran on idle deafened Brian as he was helped out of the Humvee and handed over to the airplane's crew. Red earmuff protectors, some eye shades, and a spare dark blue wool blanket were handed to Brian as the crew escorted their newly added cargo up the ramp. Inside the tremendous hold of the aircraft were crates of surplus supplies and spare parts being returned to the airbase for re-inventory.

Brian was strapped into a crew seat on the side wall of the enormous plane and offered a juice pack from a previously opened MRE meal. He looked towards the front and saw row after row of cargo crates tied down and strapped in with some large, red nylon webbing as if some mythical, large spider had sprayed her web over the boxes and crates to claim as her own. Brian then turned his attention to the rear of the craft to see outside that the soldiers and airmen were still talking. As to what they were saying, he would never know, not only because of his protective earmuffs were on, but also because the roar of the plane's engines made it also impossible.

"What the hell happened?" asked the senior load master to the Marines standing next to their vehicles.

"Whaaat?" yelled back one of the soldiers as he made the motion of cupping one ear to hear well.

"Oh, we got zapped by a handful of *Hadjis* just outside the embassy," barked back another Marine.

"Command reports they caught the other two guys, and they are being questioned now," added a military hospital orderly as he walked up with a stretcher and a few blankets.

Woods met up with the senior airman and took off his tactical glove to shake his hand. The two knew exactly what the other thought. Both took a quick glance up at Brian strapped into his seat inside the plane then, simultaneously, both looked down at the dead embassy official as he was being carefully pulled out from the back and laid onto a stretcher. An ambulance waited nearby.

"Was that douche worth it, Lieutenant?" asked the senior as he pointed with his chin towards Brian.

"It's what he wanted. He wanted to finish the mission, and I plan to honor him and get that stupid asshole back to the States. Let them figure it out," said Woods.

Within minutes, the Humvees pulled back from the runway and headed to their battalion headquarters. The military ambulance slowly drove off to the base's morgue, and the C-5M Galaxy closed its rear cargo door and taxied to the takeoff position.

Inside the cargo plane, the Air Force crew prepared for takeoff and buckled themselves in. One airman made a final inspection of Brian's harness before getting set and gave the human cargo a thumbs-up to ask Brian if he was all set.

"Yeah," Brian yelled in affirmative as he was unaware that the earmuffs he wore distorted his perception of how loud he was talking.

Up in the cockpit, the pilot and copilot both slowly moved the immense throttles of the aircraft's four huge Boeing CF6 engines forward. The C-5M slowly moved down the runway. Engines screamed; the aircraft picked up speed.

"R1. R2," droned the copilot.

As the plane passed the point of no return, also known as R2, on a runway, the pilot pulled back on the stick. The plane's nose pulled upwards, and the aircraft roared skyward. A series of six brilliant, bright orange flares ejected out of both sides of the C-5M as the copilot switched on the defensive counter-measures control panel. The flares were decoys that emitted tremendous heat as they burned like a firework on the Fourth of July. Since the attack on the embassy's passenger and convoy, the C-5M's flight crew wanted no surprises from some insurgent's anti-aircraft missile from the hills close by.

"I'm on my way home," Brian said.

As he pulled the eye shades over his eyes, Brian produced one faint, cocky smirk as he fell asleep for the long ride home.

CHAPTER 16

A Time to Build

The next day, the boys, Elizabeth, and the boys' mother finished an early breakfast. The mother was prepared for a road trip down to Savannah to meet an art gallery owner who had shown an interest in her metal sculptures.

"Okay, kids, you have plenty of food and drinks to keep you satisfied for a couple of days. Your dad is in this area for the whole week and will be home each night. Behave and try not to kill each other!" the mother said.

Mrs. Cotter gave a quick smile, kissed each one on the head, and walked out the kitchen door. Within a few minutes, her SUV was gone.

Like ducks following each other, Steve and Elizabeth stayed in step with Michael as they left the house and proceeded down the hill to the boathouse. The three then climbed into the pontoon boat, and Elizabeth went through her routine to start the engine. Steve removed the boat lines from the cleats on the dock, and the pontoon boat gently pulled away from the covered slip.

"Where to, guys?" asked Michael.

He straightened the wheel and increased the speed on the throttle. The pontoon boat sputtered and choked on the old fuel that was still in the engine from its long *siesta.*

"I don't care. It's a beautiful day. Captain's Discretion," said Elizabeth.

Michael made a course change and headed out of their hidden cove. The boat passed by an old, black and white lighthouse stationed at the end of a pier; this reduced-scale replica was merely for show. On its best days, the 100-watt bulb gave the impression of a navigational aid.

"What's that?" asked Elizabeth.

"Oh, that's the old lighthouse. We use it to help us find which is our cove," Steve said then added, "I saw Michael kiss that girl Jennifer last summer under that thing."

"Jerk," Michael protested.

As the pontoon boat cleared the entrance to the cove and headed out into the lake, the boat's engine began to skip. The fuel filter that had done its best to keep last year's gas from the engine had finally failed in its duties. The engine died.

"Oh, damn," Michael said as he tried to restart the engine.

The engine turned over, sputtered, and then died again. A few more attempts were in vain.

"Well, are we in trouble?" asked Elizabeth.

"Get out Dad's electric boat motor. You know, the one we talked about," Michael ordered Steve.

Steve opened a locker box and pulled out a heavy duty electric boat motor. It was black and had a three-blade propeller and special clamps that attached to the railing of the pontoon boat. A pair of cables trailed from the locker box to three extra-large marine batteries. Bigger than a car battery, these batteries had a long life span and plenty of reserve power.

"What if these batteries are dead? They've been sitting in this locker for over a year," Steve asked.

"Nope. Dad got new ones the other day after he went to go pick up Elizabeth. He said we could take Elizabeth fishing," Michael responded as he nodded to Elizabeth.

The electric motor sprang to life, and the boat moved forward. Michael took no chances, and he turned the ship around and headed back to their dock.

They pulled into the covered boathouse fifteen minutes later; Elizabeth helped and tied the boat up. They passed the scrap pile of metal, pipes, and the large propane tank, and Michael began to think about what to do next.

"Alright, fun day on the lake is postponed for now until the boat's engine settles down from being flooded with that old crap fuel. There's some gas in the garage. As for now, let's get to work on this," Michael said.

"What can I do?" asked Elizabeth.

"Well, you're good with engines. Get the wheelbarrow from the garage. Get the gas can, and see if you can fix the pontoon boat," Michael said.

He then turned his attention to Steve and said, "You go get Mom's welder and cutting torch."

"They're heavy," Steve protested.

Michael smiled and slapped his brother on the back, and the two walked up to the house. Their mother's studio was attached to the house, a large room filled with equipment and spare metal bottles of different gases. The bottles, shaped like standing torpedoes, were painted in green, blue, or orange, depicting what gas was stored inside. The cutting torch was the acetylene kind that required plenty of gas in a cylinder and a companion oxygen bottle as well. The special tanks were chained to a heavy duty hand cart that helped in moving the torches around. A welder's face and eye protector and thick gloves were also available close by. The welding machine was a handheld, gun-like device that attached to an electrical generator with a thick power cord. With a loose spool of welding solder, the boys had a unique tool that would weld steel together with ease. The hardest part for the boys was the immense weight of the equipment and trying to manage their bulky find down the hill to the boat dock.

Within thirty minutes, everyone was busy with their assignments at the lake's shoreline. The boys pulled the scrap parts apart and began to assess what they had and what they needed.

Michael took charge and designated himself as the chief welder and architect of the submarine.

CHAPTER 17

Don't Wake Me Up

"Mr. President, First Lady, members of the Senate and House, it is my honor and privilege to introduce Special Detective Carl Trip as the newest inductee into the FBI's highest honor for gallantry and bravery. He singlehandedly captured the terrorists who were going to destroy the dam at Lake Sydney Lanier. Carl, Carl...."

Carl awoke from his dream only to find Joyce standing over the sofa where he was napping. She tugged at his foot to get him up.

"What... what... are you doing here?" asked Carl.

"It's me Joyce. We went out on your boat and I got sick, remember? You said we would go out tonight to let me make it up you," she whispered as she bent over and exposed her pink bikini top underneath.

"I'm on a specific assignment right now, baby, and I'm broke and tired," complained Carl.

He righted himself on the beat-up sofa, spilling the crumbs out of an empty pizza box onto the carpet. Carl then ran his fingers through his hair and scratched his head. Like an old grizzly bear, he labored to wake up from a long hibernation.

"What I want is to be on your boat, find one of those secluded coves you bragged about, lay out a beach towel up front, and catch some sun. That doesn't cost money, and, besides, we could grill a hot dog for dinner," she purred into Carl's ear.

With a sudden new found vigor, Carl got up and looked for his keys. He tucked his red shirt into his shorts, pausing long enough to spank Joyce's bottom. He left his hand there long enough to check for that bikini bottom.

"Come on, babe. We are on a new mission."

CHAPTER 18

Details, Details

The large silver propane tank the boys were working on started to take shape. The gaping hole that the scrap company had cut away was the first objective. The dome-shaped valve assembly was replaced by the boys. This large, metal, box-shaped lid was welded in pieces and covered the opening on the top. This was to be the main hatch to get in and out of the sub. It took Michael a couple of tries to cut the right semicircle into the hood to fit the hull. He remembered a trick using a string and some welder's chalk to create the shape needed.

There was some rubber matting found in the scrap heap next to their mother's shop. It came from an old office building that was disposing of all of its comfort floor mats. The boys' mom had needed twenty of those mats to shred long ways to make a hairpiece for one of her giant metal statues.

With some heavy duty shears and an electric jig saw, Michael was able to cut out a hole in one of the mats. By eliminating the center, he created a large rectangular shape that looked like a large picture frame. This formed the perfect rubber washer along the edges to keep out water. A series of wing nut bolts were welded to the bottom of the conning tower pointed downwards. These bolts fit through a series of holes along the opening in the propane tank hull. Once inside, the sub driver could screw on the wing nuts. This allowed the occupant inside the submarine to seal shut the conning tower from the inside. Two old car's hatchback hydraulic arms, which looked like bicycle pumps, were installed to ease the lifting of the heavy main hatch.

The crew needed a series of heavy weights to keep the sub upright while in the water and provide ballast to help it submerge. Michael knew that this was the most important part since the hull was like a giant steel balloon. If they used their old dumb bell weights it wouldn't be enough. They needed something heavy and solid, yet it needed to be easy to release if the submarine got into trouble.

Elizabeth remembered seeing two rusted, eight-foot-long railroad rails. Those iron rails were to be used as legs for a statue and were lying under some plywood back at the mother's workshop up the hill. She put two fingers in her mouth and let out a loud whistle which caught Steve and Michael's attention. As they looked up, she pointed towards their mom's shed.

The two made it up the hill to find Elizabeth's discovery.

"What cha find?" asked Steve.

Michael nodded and smiled at what Elizabeth had found. He wanted to say that he had thought about it already, but he was very proud that Elizabeth had thought about it as well.

"Your keel, and your emergency escape mechanism," she proudly responded.

"Cut out two holes in the bottom of the sub. Weld these two rails together, and add two large bolts with nuts to hold it in place. It will help you sink and keep you balanced upright. And, if you get into trouble and are trapped on the bottom, unscrew the large nuts holding the bolts, and the sub floats to the surface like a cork," she added.

"Awesome, cousin," Michael said.

"Won't the sub leak with those two holes?" asked Steve.

"Well, it really doesn't matter if your intention was to escape a watery grave now does it?" replied Elizabeth.

The brothers quickly nodded.

Michael went off to get the four-wheeler to tow the rails down to the shore. Steve started to remove the debris that was on top of the rails.

Elizabeth put her hands on her hips and stared up into the sky like a super heroine.

"I am awesome," she softly crowed.

CHAPTER 19

Cabin Service

Brian woke up as he was tapped on the shoulder by an Air Force warrant officer. Having been asleep for the entire trip, his mouth was parched from the pressurized cargo bay. He scratched his head, rubbed his eyes, and looked up to see the officer holding a hot cup of coffee. The smell of the hot beverage was enough to wake him up.

"Excuse me, sir. Want some coffee or tea?" he shouted into Brian's ear protection.

"What's that? Coffee? Yeah, sure. Thanks."

Brian thanked the man as he took the hot cup from his hand. Sipping slowly, he pondered what would happen next. He studied the cargo hold. There seemed to be a handful of wounded soldiers and equipment being brought back to the States. No one seemed to really be watching over him.

Brian looked out of the plane's window and tried to reflect on what he had been through. It had taken several weeks to get to Afghanistan. He had travelled to Frankfurt, Germany, from Atlanta on his father's military pass. He had then caught a train to Istanbul, Turkey. From there, he had made it to the Syrian border. At the border, he had met up with some other American students who were also hoping to take up arms and join the fight with ISIS. Bunched together like a band of sloppy tourists, they had given Brian money to help translate for them. Brian had helped them as best he could and had been able to acquire food and a place for them to stay.

The Turkish authorities had arrested the group the next morning thanks to an anonymous tip from the hotel clerk. Brian had been detained but had been quickly released when the police had noticed that he was a US military dependent from his special identification pass.

The following morning, Brian had slipped away from the watchful eyes of the local police by using a series of back alleyways. He had gotten lost for a brief while until he had stumbled across the back entrance of a small apartment.

There had been an older man sitting on the concrete stoop. He had worn a head scarf that wrapped around his head and face. The part of the face that was exposed had been dark and wrinkled from too much sun. His eyes had been fierce, and he had stared at Brian like a lion that had just been tossed a piece of meat to enjoy.

Cleaning his AK-47, the man had called out to Brian as to why was he snooping around. Brian had chosen his words carefully, for he had not wanted to end up on the wrong side of the man's weapon. With a brave sigh, he had told the man in Arabic that he had come to join the struggle. Using as many colloquial phrases as he knew, Brian had attempted to totally separate himself from some tourist. He had even used the word 'Mujahedeen."

The man had stood up, and he had readied his assault rifle. He had looked at Brian carefully. With an approving nod, he had held out his hand in a gesture indicating he wanted to be paid to take him. Brian had taken the last of his money that the others had given him and had handed it over to him. Afterwards, Brian had then made an old gesture. He had raised his right hand to his heart like someone doing the pledge of allegiance. This act had impressed the guide, for the gesture meant "from and to one's heart."

The old fighter had said that he was on his way to Afghanistan. He had mentioned that the fighting had moved on from Syria and Iraq, and that the Afghan mountains were where he should go. ISIS had begun its movement there and had needed new fighters who would quickly rise up in the ranks and be a vital part in the fight. He had invited Brian to sit and enjoy some food and tea. The next morning, they had begun their journey. Sometime during the long trip, Brian had fashioned a hole under the sole of his left shoe to hide his special military pass.

Brian blinked his eyes and focused back on being inside the military plane. He rewrapped the blanket to fight off a morning chill that ran down his spine. Brian then took the coffee cup and sipped another gulp of the warrant officer's fairly good coffee and placed it the seat next to him.

A meal ready to eat, otherwise known as an MRE, had been placed by his side during the night. He opened the box and brought out the contents one by one; he ate everything. He was amazed at just how hungry he really was.

"The college kid likes that boxed crap," said one of the wounded soldiers to a flight crewman.

"Shit, he can have mine, too. My woman is waiting for me on the tarmac. And there better be a six pack of beer, my favorite smokes, and a bucket of chicken wings waiting in the car, or I'll be pissed," responded another voice from one of the wounded bunk beds bolted to the cargo bay floor.

Three stories above, on the red, LED-lit flight deck of the plane, a pilot, with his olive green Nomex glove, reached up to the command console above his head and switched on the “Prepare for Landing” light. In twenty minutes, they would be home.

CHAPTER 20

Alert!

The email arrived at Bill's computer with the usual blip sound as yet another alert was posted on the DNR Flash Alert site. The captain didn't respond to it immediately, but he gave it a glance as he was preparing to call it a day. A printer behind his desk on a credenza sprang to life as it whirred and hummed while warming up to print out the same news in paper form.

"Really? At four-forty-five on a Friday afternoon," fussed Bill.

He twirled his office chair around. His right knee hit the corner of the desk and shot sharp pain signals through his body.

"Shit!"

He grabbed the printed email message from the printer as he rubbed vigorously at his knee as it throbbed. He started to read.

FLASH MESSAGE ALERT

COMSAT 781 Notification: Alpha

SITREP: Intel has strong readings of an imminent terror attack (Level 4) on key assets such as water municipalities, storages, hydroelectric facilities, and recreational. All personnel are on a Code Orange alert status. No leave or personal time will be authorized. Senior directors are to report to Atlanta at 0830 Saturday (tomorrow).

END

"Oh, geez, maybe Carl was right?" Bill said.

He picked up the phone on his desk and dialed Carl's cell.

CHAPTER 21

Whoopsie Daisy

The boat was finally still as Carl walked back from the bow after he dropped anchor. The afternoon sun had just begun to disappear behind the pine trees that surrounded the private cove. Joyce was sprawled out down below on the settee like a cat. As Carl crawled through the companion way door, he gingerly stepped down the ladder as he looked upon her.

"My glass is empty, darling," she whispered with a wink.

This time she knew full well the trap she had set for Carl, and she noticed the pleased look on his unshaven face. The hunter had just become the hunted.

Carl fumbled nervously with the corkscrew as he frantically opened the next bottle of Pinot Grigio. He began to sweat a bit, for this was the last of the good wine. He did have a bottle of Moscato way back in the back of the boat's refrigerator. He didn't know what it tasted like, but he had been assured by the liquor store guy that ladies just love that wine.

"Do you need any help, baby?" asked Joyce as she grew impatient.

With the sound of the cork popping from the bottle, the signal of success was only matched by a follow-up cheesy grin from Carl's face.

"Viola," shouted Joyce as she clapped for her champion.

"You mean *voilà*, as in French?" asked Carl.

"I'm not too good in speaking the language, but my French professor in the community college gave me a 3.0 for the semester because he said I knew how to act French. He was very sweet to me," said Joyce.

Carl, by this time, had already handed Joyce her glass and gazed at her breasts. Like a goofy adolescent, Carl sat down next to her and started to put his hairy arm around her.

"Can you show me how good you are in being French?" Carl asked.

The two embraced in a passionate, sloppy kiss.

Carl couldn't believe his luck. He almost got fired from his job but wasn't. This woman chased him, and they were down below in the salon of his boat. Plenty of Pinot left, she doesn't seem to be hungry, and they're in a special, secluded cove.

Ah, life's good, he thought to himself as he kissed her.

Carl's cellphone began to ring as it broke up the moment.

"Dammit," he grunted.

The cell's ring tone was special for this caller.

"It's Bill, my boss. I've got to get it," he begged Joyce as he climbed up from the settee.

"What about me? This girl is very important, too," Joyce teased Carl as she flexed her shoulders.

"Hello, boss. This better be good news," said Carl into the phone. Then he added, "Uh huh. Uh huh. Yes, sir. I was right? Yes, sir. Oh, thank you, sir. Yes. On my way."

He stood there quietly for a minute. The boat gently swaying side to side as an unknown wake made its way into the cove. Dumbfounded and confused, he rehashed the phone conversation again and again.

"There is a terrorist threat on the lake. I'll be dammed," he whispered.

"“Well, babe, duty calls. I've got another mission," Carl said as he slowly spun around towards his playmate.

"Joyce?" he called out.

There, underneath the dining table attached to the settee, Joyce was passed out cold. Her wine glass, almost empty, stood on the table alone as if on guard to watch its master sleep away the wine.

Carl shook his head at his continued misfortune with Joyce. He climbed up the ladder and started the journey home to work in the morning.

"Just my luck."

CHAPTER 22

Homecoming

The rear cargo ramp began to open, rushing in fresh air, jet diesel fumes, and a faint smell of fried chicken. The mess hall for the airbase at Dobbins had prepared dinner for the airmen.

Brian, along with the wounded who were mobile, proceeded with the stretcher bearers down onto the airport's tarmac. There was no fanfare; no bands played patriotic music. There were just medics and other ground staff who helped unload the plane and refuel for the trip back to Afghanistan. Two men with weapons approached. Each man wore Military Police armbands. One had a file with passport data attached. He looked for someone who matched Brian's description.

Brian knew this wouldn't go well if he was thoroughly questioned. He had fooled everyone until now that he was the kidnapped student. It was only a matter of time.

"Excuse me, are you Peter Staub?" asked one of the MPs.

The cargo plane's massive turbine engines started to wind down, and the place got quieter.

"Who? Oh, Peter. Yeah right. Well, he's still on the plane. He got really sick after we landed. Said something about the MRE and the plane's diesel fumes did him in. It's kind of a mess. Better let him be for a spell. Excuse me. My dad is waiting for me over there."

Brian waved at a small crowd behind a fence and caught the MPs off guard. Someone in the crowd actually waved back as a courtesy. Brian smiled and waved again, and then he smiled back at the MPs. With a point of his chin, he then walked past the soldiers and headed for the arrival terminal.

"What the hell?" muttered one of the MPs.

The two soldiers then turned and started for the plane's rear cargo door. Baffled by Brian's behavior, they had to move on to check on the mysterious Peter Staub.

Inside the doorway, Brian could see some military people, waiting friends, and parents through the glass-paned windows and doors. The entire place was cleaned and polished for this reception. It smelled of fresh pine floor wax. There were two elderly civilians who were racked with fear and excitement as they bobbed and swayed to look over the crowd. They looked for their long lost son who had been taken while abroad.

Brian's approach this time was more aggressive as he purposely walked to the grieved parents. The mother, who cried tears of joy, looked deep into Brian's face as she tried to recognize her son. The father looked at Brian as well and was happy. The mother's hand reached up and touched Brian's face. There was a silent pause. Awkwardness turned to confusion, and Brian broke the silence first.

"It is so good to be home, Mrs. Staub. I'm one of the other exchange students freed. Your son is still on the plane. He didn't feel well, but he is coming soon, I promise," Brian said politely as he gently kissed the mother's cheek and smiled at the father.

With that, Brian slowly broke free of the couple's embrace and headed past other family members. He passed through the exit doors, and he afforded one more smirk as he flagged a taxi in the parking lot.

CHAPTER 23

Hard Work

The boys and Elizabeth were in full swing during the night. The sub had its conning tower hatch welded and the floor mat cut out to make a rubber gasket. The boathouse flood lights were rearranged to offer more lighting. Summer moths flew back and forth in the bright lights. A bat patrolled the twilight sky for an unexpecting feast before it got too dark.

The next big project was to disconnect the jet ski float ramp. The ramp's primary design was to keep small craft out of the lake for off-season dry storage. The ramp used pumps to add or remove lake water from two pontoons which hoisted small boats out of the water. It rested on a rack that held the pontoons in place. When the jet ski was needed, an electronic switch would be thrown to open a series of water intake valves. The metal pontoons would fill with lake water and submerge the entire rig. This allowed the jet ski, or even a small boat, to float off the rack and be on its way. The pontoons could then be filled from either CO2 bottles or through an open air filter into a compressor mounted on the slip. With their mother's supply of welding equipment and compressed gases, the sub with attached C02 bottles could, in theory, make four to five safe dives with two tanks. A sixth dive would be risky if they used too much reserved air.

Elizabeth cranked up the jet ski and backed out of the boathouse with her feet. Once clear of the boat lift, she slowly drove the watercraft to the shore and waited for Michael to wade out and climb aboard.

Steve set about the lift's restraint cables and unbolted them from the slip next to the family's pontoon boat. He unplugged the power cord and compressor. A lanyard was tied to the back end, and Elizabeth moved the jet ski into position. Michael grabbed the other end of the lanyard and pulled. The boat lift moved out from its spot and was towed to the shore near the sub.

"Why couldn't we have just moved the sub to the boathouse?" asked Elizabeth.

"Couldn't risk the sub sinking, and we need to do a lot more welding. Besides, Steve is scared of those wasps hanging around in the boathouse," teased Michael.

Everyone laughed at the tease as they dragged the boat lift onto the sand. With everything secured, the group called it a night and proceeded back to the house.

CHAPTER 24

A Fare is Not Fair

The taxi driver was leery about driving to Gainesville. Even though it was only an hour drive, he felt uneasy about Brian in the back seat.

"You better have money or plastic, my friend. This fare is going to be expensive," said the driver.

"You take American Express?" asked Brian.

"Sure do. Don't leave home without it, they always say."

Brian reached into his back pocket to pull out the dead embassy liaison's wallet he had stolen when their Humvee got ambushed in front of the airbase. Finding an AMEX card, he flashed it at the driver who looked in the rearview mirror.

The two continued small talk until they got to city's outskirts. The address Brian gave was to his old apartment. As the taxi drove into the driveway, the cab driver started his usual sad news story that he was divorced, forced out of his house, in debt, etc. The tactic worked half the time for a few more bucks in the tip.

"That will be $67.50, please, sir," said the driver as he held out his hand.

Brian handed the credit card to the driver as he leaned forward to get closer.

"I guess I need to see some identification," asked the cabbie.

Brian nodded his head and motioned like he was reaching in his back pocket.

"These days you can never be too sure, my friend," said Brian.

Brian reached over the front seat with his right hand and handed the man the credit card. Suddenly he pulled tightly on the shoulder seat belt of the driver with his left hand, pinning him to his seat. The driver was surprised by the sharp pull and looked to his left to see what had happened. Brian dropped the card in his right hand, grabbed the driver's jaw, and snapped the man's neck to the right with a violent pull.

The driver gurgled once; then his head slumped over. His eyelids remained open as his seat belt kept him mostly upright.

"My combat brothers would be impressed that I actually used one of their silent disposal tricks," whispered Brian as he climbed out of the back of the cab and moved forward.

He felt no remorse. He opened the front door and searched the front of the cab for that credit card, and he then reached under the dead man's buttocks and pulled the wallet from the dead man's back pocket. Brian turned off the engine and killed the lights. With the engine off, he pulled out the keys and used them to unlock the glove compartment. He found a zippered bank deposit bag. The contents of the bag were a disposable cell phone and some 200 dollars in cash.

Brian took both. He then went to the passenger side front door, climbed in, and cranked up the car. His left leg was on the pedals and with his left hand he steered. He slowly drove the taxi around back. The place was dark and deserted, for he knew his parents would never sell his apartment.

"Paul, you dropped off that fare right? What's your 20? Paul?" the taxi's radio sounded.

It was the dispatcher. The dead cabbie didn't mention this; he never used it. Yet, someone was waiting for a reply on the other side of the radio.

"Yeah, all done. Headed home," Brian disguised his voice as he held the radio mike near his knee to distort his voice transmission.

"Right, enjoy your couple of days off. If he paid you in cash, don't spend it. Base out," replied the gruff dispatcher.

With the taxi hidden away behind Brian's old apartment, he reached through the broken door window and let himself inside the house.

No power, no lights, not even water, the apartment's kitchen smelled of urine, stale cigarettes, and rotten food. A dead rat was half decomposed in the corner. It seemed that homeless people and prostitutes enjoyed Brian's absence.

Brian went back out and dragged the dead driver into the house. He dumped the body in the space where the old refrigerator used to be located. He then erased all the drag marks with his shoes on the floor and outside.

Brian went back inside and propped the dead driver up against the wall. With the body upright, Brian straightened out the legs and put both hands in the dead man's lap. Now the dead cabbie looked as if he passed out and died in the kitchen. For an added touch, Brian picked up a cigarette butt from the trashed floor and placed it the cabbie's fingers. Brian then found an empty beer bottle and placed it in the dead man's left hand.

"The drink is on me," he said with a sneer.

With that grisly task completed, Brian walked out, closed the back door, and drove to a local hotel for a shower, a good meal, and to finally call Anya to tell her he was home from Afghanistan.

CHAPTER 25

Lost and Found

The duty officer was in a tizzy. He knew that the boy's parents were in the waiting area looking for their son. Most of the other people had left, and the large C-5 plane had already taxied to the runway for another flight to Kabul. The phone rang on his desk, and he picked up the receiver. He paused to hear the report from the MP.

"What do you mean you can't find him?" said the duty officer into the telephone.

"That's just it, sir. Peter Staub was not on the plane. Some other student said he was barfing up an MRE and would be out in a while. We waited for about 15 minutes; then we asked one of the crew chiefs where the kid was," answered the MP.

The duty officer put down the phone and cursed silently. He gathered his composure then walked out of his office and down the hall to the greeting area off the tarmac. Telling confused parents that they have lost their son was not his forte.

"This is not in my pay grade to do this shit," he said as he walked.

The look of horror was already on their faces, even before he said another word. They had been waiting patiently on a nearby bench just down from his office. They had heard what the officer said as he came around the corner.

CHAPTER 26

Breaking and Entering

There was an uneasy feeling with the troops of the Georgia National Guard unit as they approached the chain link fence to the dam. It was 2:25 a.m. and the entire complex was eerily quiet. One soldier with a professional pellet rifle and a patch over his right eye to keep it accustomed to the dark prepared his scope for the critical shot. His fellow soldiers teased him that he needed to be in the Navy. A technical edge ages ago was to wear an eye patch. It was not because the person had lost an eye, but it was to have one eye already dilated to help him see in the dark recesses of a captured ship. The sniper took careful aim at the security light that illuminated the entrance and shot it out. The locked front gate went dark. Two Guardsmen with a heavy bolt cutter crept forward in a crouched stance and made it to the chain and padlock. With one quick snip, the chain broke free.

The Guard unit then raced on foot towards the main door of the operations center of the dam. One soldier rang the buzzer to the intercom while the others lined up in a formation known as Slicing the Pie. This was a tactical formation that resembled a stick, and it was used when breaching an entrance way. Each soldier was responsible for every angle the formation would encounter while providing the enemy with a minimal target at which to shoot back.

"You are in a secure area, and you are trespassing on government property," said an older voice over the speaker.

"This is Captain Bowler of the Georgia National Guard. The dam is under attack by a terrorist group, and my unit has come to protect the dam and to see to it that you are not in danger. Open the door, please."

The ruse worked, and the dam worker unlocked and opened the heavy steel door. The stick formation moved in quickly and captured the two workers. With no shots fired and nobody wounded or killed, the takeover happened in less than a minute. With all the rooms inside the dam searched and the computer feed from the main engineering office disconnected, the men went into phase two of their special mission.

Captain Bowler nodded to his radioman, a dairy farmer from that area, to send the prearranged success code to the governor's office. The radio antennae was pointed outside the door and the signal was sent.

"The cow has just calved," said the radioman.

"What the hell was that?" asked Bowler.

"Sorry, sir. It was from an old war movie. I thought it would be kind of cool to use."

CHAPTER 27

Back at Work

The next morning at 8:45 a.m., Carl knocked on Bill's door and stuck his head in.

"I thought you had some meeting to go to this morning?" Carl asked.

"No, they called it off, but we had a phone conference. Here is your new pistol. Sign the paperwork for it. Also, your records will not show any disciplinary action. Seems that the brass has you in the spotlight on this camera boat," Bill said.

The two chatted for about an hour as what to expect next. The biggest concern was the holiday traffic for the lake. A perfect target would be one of the marinas. The wealth of those expensive yachts and sailboats would all go up in flames if something started a catastrophic fire or explosion. The environmental hazards would be enormous as well.

"The dam—what about the dam? Can a terrorist blow it up?" Carl asked.

"Corps of Engineers says it's too big to be blown," Bill replied.

"Still, we need to keep an eye on it. My guess is it won't be us."

Bill stood up first which prompted Carl to follow suit. The two shook hands, and then Carl was on his way to his locker.

Carl was greeted by other officers in the hallway. "Welcome back" and "Great job" were the usual remarks. Carl felt a certain pride and redemption, but, deep down inside, he knew this was all started with a lie.

CHAPTER 28

The Neighbor

The ringtone of Michael's cellphone woke him up the next morning. He squinted in the early light to see who had called.

"Hey, Michael. It's me Jack. I'm back from Florida. What did ya'll do while I was gone?" he asked.

"Huh? Oh, hey, Jack. What time is it?"

"Nine-thirty. Can I come over? Dad got me a couple of things while I was down to visit him."

"Yeah, sure," answered Michael and hung up the cell phone.

Michael then rolled over in bed and quickly texted Jack back to make it 10:30.

Breakfast consisted of an instant breakfast drink and a piece of toast for Steven and Michael. As for Elizabeth, some yogurt was just right.

The trio headed to the sub and started to work. The joining of the hull to the lifting pontoons would be a difficult task.

That day also meant the attachment of the heavy rails to be used as ballast. Elizabeth's theory of how the rails could work made absolute sense. The ever-present risk of sinking and being trapped under water did cross all of their minds, especially Michael's. He had added a special touch with welded handles to the large nuts for easier turning without a wrench.

The boys had also acquired some heavy silicon-based grease. Used as a medium between two heavy objects like a fifth wheel to a trailer's hitch, it was perfect to seal small holes that had wires or rods from the sub's hull. Their mother used it to prevent welder's splash. The molten sparks that burn anything they touch were nullified by the grease, which was nonflammable.

CHAPTER 29

The News Channel

The next morning, Brian found his way to the breakfast bar area of the hotel. The usual fare was readily available. Brian hadn't shaved off his beard yet, but his hair and clothes were cleaner and no worse for wear from his long journey home.

Remaining as close to his own interpretation of Muslim culture and beliefs as he could, Brian carefully picked out fruits and yogurt for his morning meal. Some of the guests in the breakfast area quietly ate their meals as they watched the local news on the television. The littlest child of one of the families turned his chair to watch Brian eat. Brian's dark beard was an object of fascination for him.

A quick giggle erupted from the boy as Brian accidentally spilled a little yogurt onto his sleeve and hurriedly licked it off.

The mother quietly placed her hand over her son's mouth, silencing his laughter, and pulled his chair back around to face the table.

Brian ignored the commotion as he listened to the latest news report.

"This just in to our news room: the Water Wars will continue in legal debate as the three governors of Alabama, Florida, and Georgia fight over the rights to Atlanta's main reservoir, Lake Lanier. Still no word on the planned additional release of water from the Corps of Engineers' Buford Dam. The contention is that more water is needed on the Chattahoochee River to help with barge traffic, water municipalities of other cities below Atlanta, and to help preserve a species of mollusks that are indigenous to the southern end of the river where the three States border each other," said the news anchor.

He then added, "Hold on, folks. We are going live to the governor's mansion where Governor Nodell is about to make a statement on today's conference on this subject."

"Ladies and gentlemen of the great State of Georgia," began the governor.

Governor J.C. Nodell was a proud Georgian. Always dressed in a navy blue suit, white shirt, and a burgundy and navy-striped tie, he looked the part of an authority. He was the descendant of German immigrants who had arrived during the American Civil War. Those Nodells had quickly dropped the *umlaut* over the "o" in their last name. J.C. Nodell came from a long line of politicians.

"It is with a sad heart that I regret to inform you that we have not come to an agreement on the rights of our state and the rights of our sovereign water supply. We were good stewards in the mid to late 1950s to have the forethought of creating a great water reservoir to meet the needs of our capital and of the surrounding areas."

During his announcement, applause erupted in the press room at the governor's mansion for a brief moment, interrupting him. Then he continued as he looked into the camera.

"The federal government wants to intervene and mandate that we Georgians release more water for the other states. I say a resounding "No" to such an idea. We dearly love our Southern brethren, but enough is enough. Build your own water resources. Stop this nonsense, come back to the conference table with an open mind, and we will be glad to come to some form of agreement."

Another round of applause erupted.

"And to our federal government, you made a mistake once before in interfering with a state's rights. We are like that coiled rattlesnake on a goldenrod banner which says, and I quote, "Don't... tread... on... me!"

The audience went wild with thunderous applause and spirited yells and cheers of adoration for the governor's riveting speech. His voice changed to a much slower, methodical, and forebodingly dreadful tone.

"I have informed the State Senate and members of the House of Representatives, that we are within our rights to seize control of Buford Dam to regulate, if not retain, our water resources and force the great states of Alabama and Florida back to the negotiation table. Last night, the Georgia National Guard, under my command, detained the Buford Dam employees for their protection during these stressful times. The wired communication link to the flood gates has been temporarily disabled. This might seem a desperate measure on our part, but I intend to bring this matter to a quick and decisive end for the betterment of all concerned. Thank you."

The governor then turned sharply and proceeded to his limousine escorted by the blue and gray uniformed officers of the Georgia State

Patrol.

With his mouth open and in complete stunned silence, the news anchor was prompted to continue with an evaluation of what had just occurred. He stared blankly at the camera's lens. The anchor stammered and spoke just a few short and familiar words that the station would be back after a commercial break.

The hotel's breakfast area grew silent. The family of the small boy quickly got up and left. The boy still looked at Brian as a curiosity.

Others quietly left as well. Brian, however, stayed and continued to watch the news of this unusual morning start.

The hotel clerk entered the breakfast area to start the clean-up after everyone had left. He paused and asked Brian if he needed anything else.

"Yes, do you have a phone book? I want to call my old girlfriend," Brian said softly.

CHAPTER 30

Is Your Mom Home?

Jack Hammock knocked on the boys' front door at 10:25. He knocked again and again with no answer.

"Are they still asleep?" he asked himself.

Jack's impatient instincts prompted him to start around back. He walked past the piles of rusted metal plating and pipes. Jack continued to search until he saw everyone down by the boathouse.

He waved anxiously with his toys and proceeded down the hill. He made a wide berth around an old pine tree stump along the trail. Jack remembered last year's encounter with a yellow jacket nest, and he instinctively winced in pain as he remembered the three stings on his neck. He continued past the stump.

"Aw, Jack, you big baby. You still scared of those bees?" cried out Steven.

"Hey, I wasn't scared when those wasps stung me," added Elizabeth.

Michael waved his friend to come onto the dock.

"Yeah, you were a very brave girl, but Jack, there, is our local bad luck charm," Michael said.

"Hey, guys," Jack wheezed.

"Take a look at my new stuff. These are torpedoes for my family's pool. The range is really long. It uses fizzing tablets to maintain its buoyancy. When the batteries die, it unlocks a valve letting in water to four more tablets that will bring the torpedo to the surface. It's really big. My dad said it is like the torpedoes on his attack sub when he was in the Navy," Jack boasted.

The brothers and Elizabeth stopped what they were doing on the sub and approached Jack and his new toys. The torpedoes were painted a bright orange with a black front end. The reciprocal propellers were a bright red. Official-looking decals decorated the entire body. Indeed, it was a very sharp model of a modern torpedo.

The friends also admired Jack's other toys, each shaped like a sturdy plastic pineapple . Jack displayed them in the palm of his other hand.

"My new paintball grenades Dad got me," said Jack proudly.

"It explodes red paintball paint everywhere when it hits something. Watch," Jack said.

He threw one of the grenades at a nearby pine tree. With a short flight and a sharp pop like a balloon bursting, the grenade finished its flight in a cloud of red paint against the bark of the hapless tree.

"Cool!" was the collected verbal response of the group as they marveled at the effectiveness of the paintball grenade.

Michael walked off the dock and made his way over to the pine tree and brought back the grenade.

"Jack, let me see your torpedo for a second."

Michael proceeded to take the two toys and placed the bottom end of the grenade to the front end of the torpedo. He then said, "This could be fun."

CHAPTER 31

Briefing

The full DNR contingent was on full alert. Bill, Carl, and the others sat quietly around the television in the conference room watching the news about the Georgia governor's bold move to seize the dam.

"This is bullshit," cursed one of the men. Another DNR officer acknowledged the same sentiment.

"Now, fellas, we are on standby alert. Don't get riled up yet. The government is in direct talks with the governor's people. All of this will blow over in a day or two," Bill stated to his men.

"But, boss, if the Corps of Engineers doesn't do the scheduled release once a day, the lake will keep filling. Spill Over will happen in five days. It could even weaken the earthen rampart. Don't they know that?" asked one of the men sitting around the table.

"Look. I meant what I said. Cool it! Governor Nodell is just showboating for the election. This makes him look tough against the president," Bill clarified.

"Let's get a few of you to go over to the dam. Keep your distance from the Guard. Don't antagonize them. Report any changes. Thompson, you and Rodriguez, take a boat and maintain watch on the water levels. Sing out when it's full pool, plus five, and plus ten. If it reaches plus fifteen, get out and warn other boaters. The dam will be seriously under stress. Fissures, catastrophic leaks, and breaks could occur. The U.S. Coast Guard uses channel 16 for distress calls. Carl and I will monitor everything from here. Let's go, team," said Bill.

CHAPTER 32

I Just Want to Call You

Brian walked out of the hotel. He felt excited about finally seeing Anya. He wanted to surprise her, but he wanted to make sure she was at home. He took the torn-out phone book page with her parents' phone number and used the dead cabbie's cell phone and called. The phone rang three times, and then he heard her voice.

"Hello?" whispered Anya into the phone.

Brian was completely ecstatic by her voice. His heart started to beat incredibly fast. His respiration rate increased so rapidly that he was going into a state of hyperventilation, dizziness, and alkalosis. He said no words, and he gently pushed the red stop button on the cell phone and ended the call. Clutching the phone as if he held a teddy bear, Brian wiped away some tears of joy. Tears from such happiness that he completed what his love wanted him to do. The hardships and misfortunes he endured have finally come to a conclusion. He was going to be rewarded with her affection and sweet kisses.

I will see you, my love, in ten minutes, Brian thought to himself.

The taxi started out of the parking lot of the hotel and turned the corner.

CHAPTER 33

Time to Get Up

The morning sun barely penetrated her dimly lit bedroom. Pale orange and pink veils were draped as curtains onto the four bed posts. There was even a Middle Eastern lamp close by in an attempt for an Arabian tent look. Anya slowly crawled back into her bed.

"Who was that?" asked a deep, firm voice of a male companion in her bed.

"It was nothing. A wrong number, I guess," replied Anya.

"Perhaps another lover waiting his turn with you?" the Arabic male teased.

"There is no other. Only you—and your special gifts," Anya teased back.

Climbing on top of her lover, she slowly kissed his lips as she stroked back his curly dark hair. Her kisses moved from his lips as they marched invitingly from his chin then his neck to his chest.

Moans of approval emanated from the man, enticing Anya further as she moved her hand down his body like a spider's walk.

"This is what I'm in love with," she said as she twirled her fingers across his hairy chest and let show a wicked smile.

CHAPTER 34

A Balancing Act

Michael retrieved the depth and fish finder gear from the pontoon boat. More or less a sonar device, it would serve as the sub's depth control monitor. It used minimal power from the sub's batteries. The sonar piece was attached on the bottom of the hull. Data and power cords were fed through another small hole into the sub. Another quick dab of heavy lube sealed the gaps.

Steve and Jack drove up in the four-wheeler with a collection of three large marine batteries, connection cables, and a wooden cedar planter box about three feet long. A small cloud of red dust followed behind them.

"Okay, I know what the batteries are for, but are we to plant flowers inside the sub, too?" asked Elizabeth.

"It's our bench to sit on and will cover the batteries on the floor," replied Steve.

Michael cautioned his brother and Jack as to being extra careful not to create an arc or cause sparks with the battery connections. A ground wire was quickly fabricated and attached to the hull of the sub.

The next two hard tasks to be done were completed by Michael. The powerful, electric boat motor that moved the pontoon boat when the family went fishing was installed first. The propeller and its housing were removed with an Allen wrench. Then the motor and shaft were placed inside the sub. With another hole cut through in the lower rear part of the hull, the prop shaft was pushed through and sealed into place.

Michael reattached the propeller and secured the electric motor. An old, electric, portable house fan was disassembled to reclaim the back half of the protective wire cage that kept children from touching the spinning blades.

The cage piece was then spot welded over the prop shaft to prevent weeds or debris from damaging or fouling the sub's prop.

Next Michael fashioned a rudder for the sub using an old real estate sign and its metal stand that went into the ground. He fashioned a pivotal frame from some steel rods and used the two pulleys from his mom's outdoor laundry rack and some cabling. Michael was then able to steer the sub.

Soon after, four sets of brackets were welded close to the bottom of the sub near the eight-foot keel weight. These would hold the bottles.

A large, four-wheeled car jack used by their mother for heavy lifting was brought down from the shop. A plywood board was placed over the sand and rocks next to the beached sub to provide a platform for the car jack to lift the boat to its side. Two five-foot, green air cylinders were rolled underneath and attached to the newly welded holding brackets. These cylinders would supply the compressed air for the sub's buoyancy and also allow the sub to rise to the surface. Air hoses were soon attached and screwed on to activate the boat-lifting device.

Michael later used his old Russian tank commander's periscope That had been given to him by his grandfather from an old army surplus store. The dark green tube, as large as and twice as long as a potato chip can, had a rounded top and used mirrors to operate. The periscope had been used by tank commanders to look around the tank for enemy infantry. It had also been perfect for those times at the city's Fourth of July parade when the crowds proved too packed to see through but easy to see over.

The periscope was mounted into the top hatch of the conning tower. He solder welded it into place. Michael stood back in amazement at how well it would work and how good it looked for their sub to have it.

For the first time, the four noticed that they had worked as team. The submarine was taking shape and, above all, they had fun.

"Hey, guys, I know I really sound like a goober to say this, but this is really cool," said Jack.

"Yeah, man, you're right," replied Michael.

"That this is cool?" asked Jack.

"Nope, that you are a goober," laughed Michael.

They all laughed.

CHAPTER 35

Knock, Knock

Brian parked the taxi two houses down from Anya's home. His pace quickened as he snuck through to the back of the house. Her bedroom, a second-story apartment built into the house, had its own staircase. He crept up the wooden stairs quietly, only enhancing Brian's anticipation.

Like a panther approaching its prey, Brian made it to the top landing and paused before he reached for the door knob.

Laughter was heard on the inside. It was Anya. It sounded like she was happy.

"Good, the better the surprise on her face when I enter," Brian amused himself quietly.

As he reached to open her door, he noticed how sweaty his palms were. The doorknob turned quietly, for it wasn't locked. Brian knew that his Anya despised locks. They made her feel trapped in a cage.

Brian opened the door silently. What he witnessed next was beyond his comprehension. There, in Anya's bedroom, was a naked, muscular man. The man was on top of her. The two lovers did not notice Brian as he approached.

Anya's arms embraced her lover around his shoulders. The two were totally oblivious to their uninvited voyeur.

The Arabic lover looked down at Anya and relished in his triumph. He smiled as he waited for her approval. He looked into her eyes. Her large, green eyes glistened back at him with happiness—until Anya's face turned to sheer panic. Confused, the lover tried vainly to look at her as if to ask what was wrong. It was only a couple of seconds until he saw the reflected image of a man that stood beside the bed in her eyes.

One hand grabbed the male lover's chin; the other hand reached around his neck and the quick snap that followed was all that he felt or knew. He was dead before his arched body collapsed on top of her.

Anya was frozen in disbelief. Her dead lover was still on top of her. She tried to speak—shout even—but nothing could be produced with such a tremendous shock and the mind-numbing fear that overwhelmed her entire body.

"Whore," said Brian in Arabic.

He carefully controlled his voice as if back in the mountains of Afghanistan.

"Brian?" stammered Anya.

Brian acknowledged with a nod and pulled the dead man off of her. He used the stained linens to wrap him up and then left the body on the floor.

He then climbed into the bed with Anya and grabbed her by the hair; his eyes were filled with a spurned lover's rage. He lifted her forcefully and held her naked body to his. His grizzled beard rubbed against the nape of her neck. His breath was slowed as the adrenaline began to subside.

In a shaky but conversational Arabic dialect, Brian began to question her.

"Why did you betray me?" asked Brian, although he actually used the word for "you" instead of "me."

She knew what he meant. Her teeth began to chatter uncontrollably as fear coursed through her body. She knew Brian had changed. She saw a different person—a person who had changed from almost six months ago. She also knew she was in trouble. In her culture, infidelity was punishable by death. Since they were not married, she began to think she just might survive the day.

"You are a worthless bitch. Do you realize I went to war for you? I've done unspeakable things in the name of God and you. I've killed people in hopes to impress your father of my worthiness. I still see their faces in my dreams. Why, Anya? Why?" said Brian.

She sat for a minute and did not speak a word. Fear controlled her impulse to answer him. Then she started.

"I waited. I felt ashamed that I tricked you into going overseas. Father said that I could never marry you because you were born a Christian. Now, Brian, you are here. A man to be proud to marry. Father will come home tonight and see how much better you are," she said.

Anya slowly brought her delicate arm up to caress Brian's hand. Her other hand pulled up her robe to cover her, turning her body seductively to face Brian in the bed. He sat motionless to her smooth advances. Her face and hair smelled of a sweet fragrance from a perfume that he didn't recognize.

Anya now fully faced Brian. She was in her disarming feminine element.

Her lips slowly approached Brian's ear.

"Besides, I can't say no to you. You were my best lover ever," she purred to him.

"Oh, Anya," said Brian softly as he reached up with his hands to caress her beautiful face.

Her eyes were bright and wild as the morning sun finally penetrated the veils that she had strung up. His eyes melted as he looked at her deeply—not eyes of love and forgiveness but those of total despair.

Brian's sudden jerk to the left with his arms broke Anya's neck in one swift motion. She jumped in his arms for a half of a second as nerve signals from the brain to the lungs and heart no longer transmitted their timing pulses for life. The lifeless body of Anya slumped through Brian's hold and onto the bed. Brian stood up and pulled a blanket that was on the floor over her.

"We've never been to bed, you snake. I was saving myself for you!" Brian cried out.

Downstairs, Brian heard her mother come in from the morning shopping at the market.

"Anya, I'm home. I'm going to lie down for a while," shouted the mother from the kitchen downstairs.

"Like mother, like daughter," Brian muttered as he left the bedroom and went down the steps to the kitchen.

The mother came around the corner and accidentally surprised Brian.

Thinking she was already in her bed, Brian was caught off guard. The woman screamed as she tried to run for the front door. Brian tripped her as she turned and then pushed her to the floor.

Fear overwhelmed her as the fight or flight impulses were activated inside her. The end was near for the old woman, and she knew it was coming.

"Please!" she cried to Brian in Arabic.

Brian moved his arms and legs like an Amazon python holding tight to his prey. His arms twisted and made their way into that familiar neck-breaking lock he had perfected.

Anya's mother, trapped and pinned, her breathing labored from years of asthma, tried to bite her attacker, but Brian had already anticipated her move.

His legs and arms were in position to kill her quick as they firmly held the woman. She knew the moment was almost there by the way his arms were positioned around her neck, so she tried one last time to break free. She grabbed Brian's thumb and tried to pull it back to inflict enough pain to make her escape.

Brian tensed his arms to break her neck just as she tried to grab his thumb. Like a chess game, the two opponents were in a death struggle to outdo the other. Her final move was a half second too late.

The pain deflected Brian's jerk just enough that the woman's neck broke, but it wasn't a clean one.

Instantly the woman went limp as her head had broken free from her neck. The woman was dead but still technically alive as her eyes still blinked and a gurgling sound could be heard in her throat. It was an awkward twelve seconds as her body realized it was no longer going to receive any more signals from the brain and stopped all activities. Her eyes remained open as Brian untangled himself from the corpse.

"Stupid woman. I was going to be merciful! You did this to yourself!" screamed Brian in anger.

He kicked her still body in protest. He then wiped off his sleeves as if he had just been dusted. He stepped over to the front door and pulled aside a window curtain to determine if he was indeed alone.

"I'll make myself some lunch, watch some television, and wait for dear old dad. I need a better ride anyway," sneered Brian.

He grabbed the old woman's ankles to drag her away from the door, her matronly dress being pulled upwards as her body moved down the hall. Her blank eyes stared up at the ceiling as she slid along.

CHAPTER 36

Plan to Get Wet

Deep inside the regional offices of the Corps of Engineers in Atlanta, a special committee had been formed and was in a series of teleconferences with Washington. The military and a meteorological team stood by on other closed sets.

Dr. Hart, grandson to the meteorologist Colonel Robert Hart who had advised the Allied generals during World War II, talked into the camera for all to see and hear.

"Mr. President, we are certain that a Category 1 hurricane has developed to the east of the Caribbean islands. The storm has been named "Isaac"and will hit the Georgia coastline in four days. It is predicted that it will grow into a Category 2. The remnants will bring torrents of heavy rain into the North Georgia area on day six," Hart reported.

"Good God. With Gov. Nodell holding the Buford dam hostage, the flooding will overwhelm the earthen ramparts. The dam will breach," said a member of the engineers.

"All of Atlanta will be without water. Residential property destroyed. We're talking millions and millions of gallons of water. Let's tell the news people to assist in an evacuation," mentioned another.

"Mr. President, my Rangers can sweep away those guardsmen with a couple of broomsticks. Let me begin with a battle plan to retake the dam," said an Army commander on another television monitor.

The President, on the far left monitor in the conference room, could be seen as he held his head with his hands in frustration.

"Now, gentlemen, let me be perfectly clear. I do not want bloodshed with our own countrymen in the South. No press reports to cause panic.

Let's keep this tight. We will find a political solution to this problem in four days. If not, and if Hart over there is right, I will call in our forces to open those floodgates," said the President.

"Captain Gillette, what is the status of the lake?" asked another official.

"We will be at full pool by noon tomorrow, sir," he answered.

CHAPTER 37

It Has Adjustable Seats

After lunch, the submarine received some more vital parts from the young group. A battery-operated fan to circulate the sub's inside air was mounted in the back. Steve had come back from the local boat supply place. He had purchased several large butter-sized tubs of specialized white soda and salt. Originally designed to be a dehumidifier for all types of watercraft that had a cabin, these tubs would act as "scrubbers" to help keep down the carbon dioxide buildup. It would also help reduce the humidity inside of the sub.

Steve also added some chair caster's from an old office chair that their dad had in storage. He mounted the wheels to the planter box covering the sub's bank of batteries. In doing so, the sub driver could glide forward or backward on the rolling seat. This shifting of the weight balance would offer the sub a means to dive downward or climb upward.

Jack, in the meantime, had successfully attached his paint grenade to the motorized toy torpedo. After finding a larger pipe, he had Steve weld the pipe to the front end of the sub. The new torpedo fit snuggly into its new home. A piano wire trigger was created and attached to the on/off switch of the electric motor for the torpedo. The wire went to the front end of the sub where a small hole was made in the hull. Then the hole was plugged with the welder's paste.

In this configuration, the sub's commander could aim the torpedo by moving the sub left or right. The periscope was really going to be needed for this operation.

A few hours later, it was Michael's turn to go to the local hardware store for supplies. He had the most important thing to purchase: gray paint. When he returned, Steve looked up and smiled at his big brother. Their submarine was to have its very own color.

Michael and Steve wanted to paint the sub a dark gray, much like the German U-boats of both World Wars. Their love of history and playing soldier has led to this monumental endeavor.

"What do we call her?" Elizabeth asked.

Michael seized the moment and said, "We'll call her *Wolf*. She's gray, mean-looking, and with Jack's torpedo, she's an attack sub. Yep, *Wolf*."

Steve then added, "The conning tower should receive a special marking, like a white stenciled drawing of a wolf's head to adorn its sides."

"I want to paint the wolf head, guys."

Everyone acknowledged Elizabeth's request.

CHAPTER 38

Carl Gets His Wish

"Well, Carl, looks like we'll be famous after all. The terrorists can wait. We got ourselves a crazy governor," Bill said as he changed the conference monitor to the news channel.

"Fine by me. Can I go back to my boat? I had to end my date early because of all this."

"Yeah, go ahead. Be back here tomorrow morning on time," Bill said.

As Carl walked out of the office, Bill started to think about this series of events. He had heard the news from Hart that a huge storm was on its way, but to him, it seemed years away. Bill reached into his pocket and grabbed his pack of cigarettes as he headed out the back door for a long smoke.

CHAPTER 39

Double Parked

The doorbell rang twice, awakening Brian from a short nap in the father's recliner. Brian quietly got up and tip-toed to the front door to peek through the curtains and see who was there.

"We know you are in there. This is the police. Open the door. We want to ask you some questions," sounded the policeman through the door.

Brian froze in fear. He desperately pondered how the officers could have known to come there. Did the old lady have some alarm system? Was Anya still alive and called the police? These thoughts raced through his mind.

Brian started to think about how to escape. There were bodies everywhere. He tried to think some more.

"Mr. Moori? Open the door, please," commanded the second officer followed by another knock on the door's window.

"Moori? They might think I'm a relative," said Brian.

He opened the front door slowly and smiled at the officers.

"Little... uh... Eng... English," stammered Brian.

"Uh, yes, sir. Sorry to bother you. Do you know anything or anyone related to that taxi parked a few houses down?" asked an officer.

"It matches a description of a taxi stolen yesterday. Is it yours?" inquired the other.

"No, no. Taxi no me, no," Brian replied as he bowed his head to the officers in humility.

The two officers stood quietly and looked at Brian. One of them even tried to peer over Brian's head to see inside. The uncomfortable pause seemed like an eternity to Brian. His heart pounded very hard. He even feared that the policemen could hear his chest as it thumped.

"Let's go. This guy doesn't know anything," one of the officers said.

The two officers turned and started down the steps of the house. Brian patiently waited a few seconds before he slowly closed the front door.

"Hey, hey! Wait a second," yelled an officers as both men spun back around.

Brian, sensing this might very well be his end, slowly reopened the front door and poked his head back out.

Both officers, in a half jog, bounded up the steps in unison towards the door. Brian braced his foot behind the front door in preparation to slam it shut. His hidden right hand firmly grasped the doorknob.

"Wait, don't close the door," ordered the closest officer.

Brian let out a pathetic whelp of acknowledgement and stood still. His fear returned with a vengeance to his frightened body.

"Take this card. If you see anyone or anything, call us right away," panted the other officer.

Brian slowly reached out and took the card, bowed again and closed the door. After the door closed and the officers had walked away, he let out a long sigh of relief. His pants' leg, left shoe, and the wooden floor where he stood were wet with his urine.

CHAPTER 40

The Wolf's First Steps

Jack made a move to climb into the newly painted sub. Michael quickly told him not yet and gently moved Jack to the side of the dock. Michael then grabbed a rope and tied one end to the sub's two lifting hooks on top. Originally, the hooks were used by the propane company to help lift the large tank off the delivery truck. The hooks were now vital to help raise, lower, and maintain the sub's balance when boarded. Michael then threaded the other end of the rope through the overhead crane in the boathouse. A few of the resident wasps stirred in protest around their nest in the ceiling.

Jack's attempt would have tipped the sub too much to the left. That action could have possibly capsized the sub and ruined all that they had worked for.

Michael climbed aboard and sat down on the sliding box inside. He instructed the others to hold on to the rope and pull tight if the sub was in trouble. The winch would do all the heavy lifting.

With a walkie-talkie, Michael clicked the talk button and did a voice check. Steve acknowledged it worked.

"Well, here she goes. I will back out ten to fifteen yards, so give me plenty of slack. I'll flood the ballast tanks to make her go under then blow the tanks and pitch upward. If it all goes right, I'll be back in the slip. Okay, everybody?" asked Michael.

Michael pulled the conning tower over his head. The gas struts from the old hatchback worked great as they reduced the weight of the heavy top. The wing nuts were then tightened to seal Michael inside.

"*Wolf* ready to motor out. Over," said Michael into his radio to Steve.

"Understood. Base standing by to assist," replied Steve.

Both brothers knew that staying in character added to the realism of the adventure. Their submarine was about to make its first dive. The air around the boat house was full of tension as the sub was slowly lowered even more. The sub began to float on her own as the two lifting ropes slackened. Steve and Jack began the task and removed the rear line and gave plenty of slack to the bow line.

Michael put the electric boat motor in reverse. Unfortunately, he sat too far forward on the sliding box seat. This caused the sub's bow to point downward and the back prop to chop at the surface as the *Wolf* moved backwards. Lake water sprayed everywhere from the propeller with a baptismal-like spray of relief.

"Hey, Michael, slide back a bit on the seat box. Your prop just splashed us," Steve said.

In a few seconds, the hull rocked backwards, and the prop went under, giving the sub its needed propulsion. The rudder made from the real estate sign worked fine. The submarine eased backwards slowly.

Steve, Elizabeth, and Jack all cheered in excitement as the *Wolf* took its first steps.

Michael eased off the reverse and stopped. He next began to turn two blue, outdoor-faucet-like valves to the left. This opened the inlets that let the lake water into the ballast tanks. Multiple bubbles and hisses sounded as the sub began to slowly dive.

Then it stopped. There were no more bubbles, but the sub was only partially submerged. Michael picked up the radio and called Steve.

“I'm okay. I guess I'm not heavy enough to counter the buoyancy of the hull. I will come back. You guys pull me in as well.”

Michael closed off the ballast valves. He then did a partial blow of the tanks as he released some of the compressed air that was stored in the green tanks below the hull next to the keel.

More hisses sounded followed by some bubbles. The sub began to rise. Michael nudged the throttle forward a bit to engage the electric motor. He could hear the prop as it turned. The sub crept forward with the help of the tow from the boathouse and the prop.

He pulled back and forth on the rudder cable and made the sub wiggle in the water like a lazy catfish in a pond. As the crew hauled the submarine in, Michael opened the conning tower to discuss the group's next plan.

"Change of plans. Steve, you climb in with me. Elizabeth, you take the walkie-talkie and run topside duties. Jack, assist Elizabeth," he ordered.

As the sub pulled in, Steve climbed aboard. With the awkwardness of the layout, Steve sat down with his back to Michael and faced the rear of the sub. His legs straddling the electric boat motor and drive shaft.

The two brothers tested the seat with wheels. They glided back and forth and were satisfied that the trim of the boat could work. They then closed up and motored their way backwards as before.

"Elizabeth, can you hear me?" asked Steve into the radio.

"Yes. Are you the new radio man for the *Wolf*?" she replied.

"Tell her we are prepared to make a test dive," Michael said over Steve's shoulder.

"Did you hear that, Elizabeth?

"Got it. Good luck. Surface crew standing by. Over," Elizabeth responded.

As before, Michael opened the ballast tank valves on the sides. Both tanks immediately took on water. The boys shifted the seat forward, and the sub started a slow downwards dive. From inside, they could hear the lake water washing up the hull then past the conning tower. Soon the whole sub was almost totally covered in water. Steve reached over and touched the side of the hull. The conning tower and the hull started feeling colder as the water chilled the metal.

The wing nuts used to clamp the conning tower to the hull popped and protested as pressure from inside vainly tried to escape.

"Not too deep," whispered Steve as fear began to creep into him.

Michael shoved a backwards shoulder into Steve's back as an acknowledgement. He then looked through the periscope and watched the water wash over the top of the conning tower. Then the periscope's vision turned a dark green.

"We're under," Michael said.

Within a few seconds of Michael's announcement, two leaks started. The first leak was around one of the wing nuts which held the conning tower in place. Michael quickly tightened the wing nut harder and stopped the first leak.

The other leak came from a seam where one of the cables used to steer the sub had been attached. Steve was able to plug the leak using a towel dabbed with the blue grease and his foot to apply pressure.

"I got that leak with my shoe, but it's still leaking a little. Can we come up?" asked Steve.

"You did? Great. Okay, let's come up."

With the air valves opened again, compressed air blew out the water in the ballast tanks. The boys gently rocked backwards on the seat, and the motor was accelerated. The sub rose quickly and came to the surface. Elizabeth and Jack started to haul in the rope to bring the submarine into the dock.

Michael opened the conning tower, which accidentally allowed some of the lake water to come into the sub. It got both boys slightly wet. He left the top open to let in some fresh air.

Both brothers absolutely beamed with happy emotions from the *Wolf* having had a successful first dive. The leak in the back was fixed, and a fresh line of grease was squirted on the entire rubber gasket that fitted between the conning tower and hull.

Elizabeth tied the sub to the dock's cleat. She then went over to the pontoon boat and retrieved a small plastic bag filled with odd-shaped, orange plastic plugs. The plugs were used by boaters if they hit something and their hull was breached. Hammering the plug into place stopped most holes. She tossed the bag into the sub.

Jack started to show signs that he wanted to be next in the sub. Elizabeth, as well, wanted her turn on board.

"Let Steve and I do a few more runs to make sure everything works right. In the meantime, both of you go to Mom's shop and bring down another one of those green oxygen cylinders. Use the four-wheeler and get some bottled water, please," Michael said.

Jack and Elizabeth went on their mission. Both grumbled under their breath as they scampered up the bank. Michael started to examine the pontoon boat for its next mission, and Steve wiped up the excess water inside the sub.

At the top of the bank, Jack pushed the chair on a homemade swing set built by Mrs. Cotter. He kept pushing the swing higher and higher until he let it fall behind him. The metal swing was made on a whim when she first started welding. The frame was only six feet wide by six feet tall. It was originally built for Steve when he was very young.

Michael heard the chair on the swing rock back and forth, its chains making a slight metallic screeching from the light rust. Metal against metal—it wasn't pretty. He even laughed a bit when the seat swung back and almost hit Jack in the back of the head.

"Steve, let's go. Your old swing is going to be a part of a trapeze act," he said.

CHAPTER 41

Make Yourself at Home

Brian calmed down after the police visit. He was relaxed enough to doze off in the chair. The television was still on the news channel as it reported Hurricane Isaac was now a Category 2 in the Caribbean. Reheated pizza from the microwave had filled the living room and kitchen with the smell of pepperoni and pork sausage, something that was very foul to the Muslim faithful.

Outside, a car door closed and footsteps were heard coming up to the front door. Brian awoke with a start when the front door opened. He quickly hid. Mr. Sanjeev Moori entered his house cautiously. His business suit was a necessary evil to wear. He looked forward to changing clothes and relaxing. Suchita, his wife of 24 years, usually greeted him at the door with a smile and a cup of strong, hot tea. The wet spot on the floor was an unpleasant surprise to Sanjeev, as this was totally unusual. The house smelled of pizza, the television was on an American channel, and his chair was empty but in a reclined mode. These things triggered alarms in his mind that something was terribly wrong.

"Suchita?" he called for his wife. He then added, "Anya?"

Mr. Moori walked to his chair and picked up the remote to turn off the TV. He used his other hand and felt a warmth in the seat. Someone was just there. He started to turn around and head back to the front door but was blindsided by a fist which hit him in his right jaw and stunned him. He began to regain composure but was quickly entangled by his assailant. An intruder was in his home!

The arms of the assailant held their two bodies together in a tight death struggle. It looked similar to a high school wrestling match as Brian tried to move into his favorite position. No words were spoken, but the shuffle of shoes on the hardwood floor and the occasional sounds of fists and hands that rubbed and slapped each other could be heard. Brian was surprised that Mr. Moori was physically in great shape and had begun to take control of the fight. Brian then faced Mr. Moori, and their eyes met.

"Brian," Sanjeev gasped.

The shock of this foolish boy from months ago overwhelmed him. More than six months had passed, and this boy had been long forgotten. Stunned and frightened, Moori pleaded with Brian to spare him.

"Brian! Brian, I see that you have become a fighter, a Struggler. Please stop for a moment and hear what I have to say. I am a secret fighter for ISIS. You have seen our successes in Syria and Iraq. You see, we are carrying the fight to all parts of the globe. Our recruiting videos are bringing in young people every day to join our righteous cause. You can be an inspiration to them. You, Brian, you."

"Enough, old man. You're stalling," Brian said.

"My mission is to destroy the water treatment plants for Atlanta. Join me, Brian, and we can do many great things."

Brian released his hold on Moori. The two breathed a sigh of relief from the heightened tension. Both, however, kept their hands up ready to engage again if necessary.

"Below, in my basement, I have tried a few experiments to make the waters of the lake deadly. If the plan works, the authorities would not dare open the flood gates. There is a powerful hurricane coming this way. And if the timing is right, I will release this weapon and threaten this entire region for years to come. The dam will break under the immense pressure of the swollen lake, and if it doesn't break, my special weapon will do its work and achieve similar results."

"Do you have a dirty bomb? Like a nuclear one?" Brian asked.

"We have made several attempts to bring in deadly snails from Nigeria. Our contacts in Miami and in California have been caught smuggling them in. The problem is that they are huge and easy to spot."

"Snails?" Brian asked.

"My wife and I have successfully bred a new snail, just as dangerous as the Giant but smaller. They eat anything organic, and their slime is corrosive and contains nematodes which, when in contact with humans or animals, cause meningitis. These snails are very prolific and can lay thousands of eggs and live up to eight years," Moori said.

Both paused for a second as the weight of the conversation began to take hold.

"Where is my wife?" Moori asked. "Suchita? Where are you?"

Moori walked passed Brian into the hallway and discovered his wife on the floor, motionless.

“You killed her? Why? She was my partner!. It was her biological science that made this weapon possible. You bastard! You killed my Suchita.”

Before Moori could turn around to face Brian, he was grabbed from behind by his assailant.

The horrible sound of Sanjeev’s neck as it broke was heard. Then the sudden exhale of the dead man signaled the struggle’s end.

"Welcome home, Pop."

Mr. Moori’s body hit the floor. The sound made a heavy thud on the living room floor.

With Anya and her family now disposed of, he was able to relax. As he sat in the father's recliner, Brian turned back on the television with the remote.

The news was now on an Arabic-speaking channel. Moori had programmed the TV to default to this station when turned on. The usual propaganda played on how the fighters of Afghanistan, Syria, and now Iraq had taken up the cause and how the followers of ISIS had defeated the imperialists. The reporter's monotonous drone changed as he was handed a bulletin from a producer.

Shouts of praises from the news anchor erupted as he made a plea to all who were watching that channel.

"Rise up and take arms against the American and Canadian dogs here at home! Fight!" he cried in Arabic.

The anchor began to tell a story that an entire American battalion of troops were killed that day in fighting south of the Afghan capital. His eyes were wild as he continued to read the memo aloud.

Brian sat in the chair and started to cry uncontrollably. He wiped his tears on his sleeves and cleared his throat. He knew very well that the story the news anchor had read was totally fabricated, but he still felt alone and no longer in control of his destiny.

"I can’t believe this. All that I’ve done for nothing. All I feel is just pain. Oh, Anya, why did you do this to me?" he cried.

CHAPTER 42

Where's Joyce?

Carl drove to the marina and made his way to his boat. As he entered the companionway hatch of his boat, there was no sign of Joyce.

He proceeded to the galley and found a handwritten note on a drink napkin. It was from Joyce. She wrote that she was sorry, but she had to go back to town. He reached into his pocket and pulled out his cellphone.

"Hey, babe. Come by for breakfast tomorrow. Let me make it up to you. Crazy about you." Carl left the message on her voice mail.

Carl untied his boat and motored out. It was a fine day, but that weather report had talked about some very tough days ahead.

As he turned with the wind at his back, the breeze caught the smells which emanated from the holding tank below. The commode, or "head" in nautical terminology, was full. Carl smelled the foul odor, which made him pull up his shirt to cover his nose. The boat changed course and headed to the pumping station of the marina.

After he pumped out the holding tank, Carl filled the boat up with gas. He then went into the marina store on the dock and picked up a-six pack of beer and a bottle of wine for Joyce later. The male cash register attendant that took Carl's money gave Carl the male version of "good luck" with a tired wink and a nod of approval. Carl proudly picked up his bag of goods and headed back to his boat.

CHAPTER 43

More Than Friends?

The pontoon boat now had the swing on it. Michael and Steve removed the winch from the roof of the boat house and connected it to the swing set.

Elizabeth and Jack returned with the supplies and some simple sandwiches that she had made for everyone. Jack passed some bottles of water around, and they all ate a quick bite. Steve amused himself as he tossed in pieces of bread to watch some local ducks eat a quick lunch. A lazy, green-and-blue-scaled carp nibbled on whatever sank his way.

After lunch everyone busied themselves on the pontoon boat. They pulled up the carpet and disconnected the forward floor plates. This gave access to the lake for the submarine to be transported.

With the new winch and removed floor plates, the pontoon boat became the floating base for the *Wolf*. They also fabricated two wooden slats that would be placed underneath the sub. With this configuration, the sub could travel topside over great distances on the pontoon boat. Also, the boards helped because the *Wolf* would swing wildly on the trapeze if not securely parked on the deck.

Hoisting the sub up and down by the winch was actually better for the dive tests, with one test actually going twelve feet deep. That one was with Jack in the back seat. Elizabeth got to go down twice, but she later declined any more trips to the bottom.

A new dehumidifier tub was put in to replace the other one that was full of water. Battery life was still great since the sub was using the winch more to raise or lower the hull.

The swing set used as a crane proved to be a success. The crank on the winch was well-lubed and turned easily when completing the needed tasks.

The crew also discovered that the pontoon boat had the responsibility to maneuver to the left or right to capture the *Wolf* as it rose. A few times the sub had come up sideways, causing confusion, panic, and scratches on the conning tower's paint job. The engine of the pontoon boat was in the back, and everyone knew the dangers of moving too far forward over the submarine.

Later that afternoon, the *Wolf*, piloted by Michael and with Steve manning the rear of the sub, motored out from the pontoon boat and practiced using Jack's torpedo. The group wanted a target on which they all could see the red paint grenade explode. The closest and easiest choice was the neighbor's boat house. The four massive, black plastic boxes that floated the boat house were stationary and could easily be washed off if there was too much red paint.

Michael submerged the submarine just enough so that only the periscope showed above the waterline. Looking like a green stick protruding out of the water as the *Wolf* moved, the sub's lone eye spied its intended target. The forward motion of the periscope slowed and then stopped as Michael brought the craft to a standstill.

Jack and Elizabeth watched intently from the idle pontoon boat's railing. The green periscope was about fifty yards to the left of the boat house. Jack attempted to draw an imaginary line from the periscope to the target to predict the path of his torpedo. Elizabeth tried to do the same.

"There's the torpedo," Jack said.

Elizabeth looked up to find Jack pointing at some bubbles and a curious wake that streamed towards the right front plastic float of the boat house. It looked like an orange and green fishing lure just underneath the waterline being reeled in for another cast.

"Oh, I see it now," she said.

Inside the sub, Michael's pull of the wire lanyard caused the grease plug to come out from the hole in the hull. Lake water squirted through the pea-sized breach and everything started to get wet. Instinctively, Michael reached up and placed a hand to stop the leak.

"Gimme those orange plugs Elizabeth gave us in that bag over there."

Steve reached down to the floor, produced the bag, and retrieved a rubber-like plug. Michael took the plug and crammed it well into the hole. His action finally stopped the water coming inside.

"When we get back, that will be an easy fix," Steve said.

Michael acknowledged and returned to look through the periscope. He did so just in time to watch a huge splash as compressed air and a fine mist of red paint splattered against the large float. The torpedo actually worked. The tiny electric motor that powered the torpedo cut off, and the seltzer tablets inside were exposed to the lake water. The bubbles quickly filled the torpedo, and it gently rose to the surface.

Michael and Steve brought the *Wolf* to the surface. Elizabeth motored the pontoon boat over for Jack to fish his torpedo out of the water using a fishing net on a pole.

The conning tower's hatch sprung open, and Michael and Steve beamed with excitement. Both boys had gotten their shirts wet from the small leak. Steve was just happy to have the hatch opened while still in the lake.

"That was so awesome," Michael said.

"Yeah, we saw it hit," replied Elizabeth.

The day's experiments were a success and had come to a close. Everyone had had a chance to enjoy the sub and experience the result of their hard work in building the sub.

Michael's cell phone rang. The look on his face was one of joy yet dread. He showed that half smile and frown to everyone.

"Who was it?" asked Elizabeth.

"It's Dad. He's home and wants us to clean up our mess. He said the kitchen was a wreck."

A combined moan came from the crew as they prepared to motor back to the dock. The *Wolf* was brought on board and tied down securely. The pontoon boat's motor came to life, and the group headed back to their dock.

"Jack, you're welcome to spend the night since you helped with the cleanup. Better call your mom," Steve said.

Jack nodded in agreement, but he was secretly upset that nobody let him launch his torpedo. He pouted and fidgeted enough to catch Elizabeth's attention.

"Are you okay?" she asked.

She touched Jack's arm in a tender way. He never had a girl like him, much less look at him. He felt warm inside. He then looked at her.

They were connected in some sort of way, yet neither knew of the other until a short time ago. Perhaps that they were not part of the Michael and Steven pact. Jack had always been welcome at their house until their mother would get agitated that his visits had turned into days. Last year she had actually told him to go home on the third night of a sleepover. Since then, Jack had always been leery of too long of a visit. Sometimes he would even ask Steve or Michael if their mother was home before he came over.

"Can you get away tomorrow and take me out on this boat? I want to show you something that will be fun. First, I need three heavy sandbags," he said.

Elizabeth felt warm inside, for she was intrigued that someone had noticed her and that she was liked. She admired Jack's freckles on his cheeks. Almost spotted like a Cocker Spaniel's face, Jack had a cuteness about him that Elizabeth couldn't ignore or resist.

The two shared another glance, and then Jack extended a finger of his right hand across the rail. He did so secretly as not to alert the brothers and hooked Elizabeth's little finger. She looked at him sweetly. Then they touched hands. Her excitement grew, as well as her bravery, and she reached over and held Jack's hand on top of the boat's railing.

CHAPTER 44

The Unfinished Basement

Brian finished watching the news. He then proceeded to drag the mother and father down the stairs into the basement. The hallway's Persian rug made the job of dragging the bodies downstairs easier. The rug muffled the thumps as the dead bodies dropped and bumped with each step on the stairs with a grizzly rhythm.

Once down in the basement, Brian started to look around as to what was there. The entire basement smelled of a powerful, putrid, earthlike odor that burned his eyes and throat a bit. A fan placed in a closed-off window blew most of the noxious fumes outside.

In the corner of the basement were five metal vats normally used for keeping live fish bait. Each vat was connected to a water filtration and aerator system. The heavy devices were placed on the cold concrete floor to keep alive the mysteries in the dark swirling water. Brian picked up a mesh scoop that had been placed on the corner edge of one of the vats and hauled up what was in the vat. To his surprise, he held thousands of tiny floating snails in the strainer. Like an evil bowl of cereal, the snails twirled in the conditioned water. Some were dead, but the majority were alive and feasting on their deceased comrades.

"Is this your weapon? These snails?" Brian asked the facedown body of the father.

There was a metal cabinet nearby the vats. As Brian opened the doors, he noticed cases and cases of freeze-dried shrimp egg pellets used by fishermen and pet shops to feed small aquatic fish. By quick count, he figured that there were at least twelve cases. Some old receipts lying around showed that Anya's father had been slowly buying his collection of freeze-dried shrimp eggs and boxes of fish food for a year from various pet stores.

There were other things of interest as well. A large pair of industrial gloves, heavy duty fans, several of those eight-foot plastic pipes used in draining and irrigation, a long eight-inch gutter placed on top of a couple of saw horses, and five one-gallon buckets. It appeared that each of the five holding vats had its own tube, bucket, strainer, and supplies. One bucket that had been filled already with the shrimp eggs stood alone off to the side.

Then he noticed a map. It was a street map of Hall County, and it was folded in half. The wrinkled map was taped up on a wall, showing only Buford Dam, Lake Lanier, and the surrounding property. A handwritten chart was close by with lake levels recorded for every day of that month right up until the day before.

There was a TV on a cart. It had a DVD/DVR player idling on pause. The screen on the television was dark as the screen saver had activated on its own.

Curious, Brian picked up the remote and pressed the play button. The TV set blinked a few times and started to display Sanjeev Moori talking about what he had created in the family basement.

Brian sat down in a chair nearby and waited for the recording to play. He watched in detail as Moori outlined his wife's research, his method of attack, and the devastation he would create. What he saw and heard next sent a chill down his spine.

Moori was indeed secretly a fighter for ISIS, a fanatical group of Islamic extremists that had caused a regional spread of terrorism throughout the Middle East. There was a black flag half curled on its staff that was Moori's "Black Flag of Jihad," known to Western observers as the *Rayat al-uquab*, or "Banner of the Eagle." It was a leftover symbol copied from the Roman Empire in ages past during their occupation. This was a familiar symbol when other Jihadists, like ISIS, attacked. Moori belonged to a secret cell within the Georgia community designed to cause havoc when called to do so. Military and civilian targets of opportunity would be the Centers of Disease Control. or CDC, now fighting the Ebola virus; railroad hubs that connected in Atlanta and American industry; and even the water treatment plants surrounding Atlanta.

"I thought Anya was of another religious sect?" Brian whispered to himself.

Brian quickly realized that Moori had been living two lives. He had allowed his wife and daughter to live and look the part of a westernized Muslim family, thus concealing his secret identity. In reality, Moori had despised the vile acts of vanity in which his family lived, a lifestyle which his true religion would someday wipe clean. Other parts of the tape on this subject were denouncements of Anya's clothing, music, and education. The wife was spared such verbal denouncements, but he did mention that he admired her education in Biology.

Brian was not totally fluent in Moori's colloquial use of the Dari language mixed with English, but he could still make out that the snail experiment was an ecological weapon and that Moori was determined to carry the fight to this country. The target was Lake Lanier, and the weapon would be the small snails that Moori had successfully smuggled into this country.

The snails were named scaegrot, which actually meant "Old Red." They were known in South America by locals in the Amazon River basin and pronounced "skagrot." This name originated from a German-Dutch explorer who was surveying that part of the river basin for raw materials for Europe. Average by snail standards, these snails multiplied rapidly. It was their numbers that made them deadly. Their main food was aquatic plant life, algae, and slime. They were prolific eaters and could be very mobile. The snail could retain methane from its digestive system and force gas into its shell. This allowed the snail to release its hold and float along the currents like a dandelion seed floats along on a warm breeze. When it was ready to land, it would simply burp out the gas and sink.

The snail's by-product was a reddish slime that looked like rot. This form of acid was corrosive to carbon-based materials. When a rout, as a colony was called, worked together, destruction came *en masse*. Whole villages were destroyed, and thousands of acres ruined each year as the snails devoured the river's vegetation, infected fish and humans, and threatened the entire ecosystem.

Moori's attack would be aggressive. He had acquired an old septic tank truck from a local plumber who just went bankrupt. With the truck loaded with his immense batch of snails, Moori would ram the barbed wire fence that protected the earthen part of the dam. An old service road ran the length of the dam with no concrete pylons to slow an aggressor. He then could get close to the concrete part of the dam. The truck's disguise would look like some septic work being done, albeit the truck was driving too fast.

Moori had also noted that the dam made a routine discharge of over 375 million gallons of lake water every day at 2:55 p.m. Those releases kept the dam stable from too much water pressure, while it provided the valuable resources. It was also to keep the Chattahoochee River at safe levels for recreation, water resources, and navigational traffic downstream. Not risking his special batch on the little trickle that came from the dam, Moori needed the snails to travel downstream in fast, fresh, oxygenated water towards Atlanta and further targets downstream. The full swell of a discharge would ensure that most of his deadly weapon would make it to the Atlanta suburbs. As they settled in the small pools and still waters of the Chattahoochee River, they would begin their feasting upon all life in the river. The shrimp eggs would be released next to act as a catalyst downstream, renewing the snail's vigor and multiplication. To some, the snail's actions might be extremely small to such a vast body of water as the Chattahoochee River. However, the scaegrots had no predators in that part of the world and could multiply over time and wreak havoc completely unhindered.

Their toxic wastes being discharged into the river would cause further damage for years to come. Since their excrement was corrosive to carbon materials, any water treatment plant's filtering system would easily begin to fail as the scaegrots and their rot deteriorated their usefulness. The diseases that they could spread would add to the terror. The snails enjoyed eating rat feces and could contract a disease called rat lungworm. This parasite could enter a human or animal and make its way to the brain of the infected host.

Moori had bred the bean-sized snails in small batches to observe the growth rate and consumption rate of materials. He had discovered that freeze-dried shrimp eggs, almost like fine sand to human eyes, was an aphrodisiac to the snails, creating not only an eating frenzy, but also making them aggressive and propagate at an extreme rate.

The video included release-time tables of the water, locations of the release drains on the dam, and how he would deliver this special weapon. The snails could survive out of the water for eight hours by making itself a mucus plug at the opening of its shell. He had also noted that the scaegrots were very flammable since their internal organs produced methane gas when they digested their meals.

Further in the recording was a film made somewhere on a deserted lot where Moori had experimented the burning of just 20 of those small snails. The fireball from the explosion had singed Moori's eyebrows. Also on the recording was a warning to always have the fans running as an exhaust for the dangerous fumes.

Moori also revealed a tragic study that was to his advantage. A team of biologists had died trying to help the people in the Amazon basin to fight the scaegrots. An experiment which used a chlorine spray quickly killed the snails. However, the combination of the sulfur-like enzymes of the snails, coupled with its waste of an ammonia byproduct, and finally with the chlorine spray, created a toxic cloud of poisonous gas. This was similar to the poison gas called Mustard Gas used with great lethality by both sides in the First World War. This gas needed three key ingredients: chlorine, ammonia, and sulfur.

This discovery would be helpful if the authorities tried to destroy his eco-weapon. A more promising note to Moori was the fact that all of Atlanta's water treatment plants used chlorine to treat the raw waters of the Chattahoochee River. The technicians running the plants would likely be killed by the toxic fumes, and thus it increased the terror by key personnel being incapacitated. Even if the water treatment plants shut down production of fresh water, the lack of water to the thirsty cities along the river, which included the ones in Alabama and Florida, would be simply horrible to commerce, life necessities, and even recreation.

Moori mentioned briefly that if the authorities tried to reduce the water in the river to kill the scaegrots, the dam would undergo severe stress levels at emergency full-pool or even at spill-over levels. With the Buford dam critically weakened, the entire water system for this region would be in chaos for years to come. Sixteen dams had failed all across the world since 2008 due to heavy rains or other conditions which overwhelmed the structures

"This is incredible," Brian said.

There was another section on the video where Moori made a dry run to the dam on a rented boat. With the video camera placed in a chair and a towel over it to hide it, Moori had driven back and forth to find a way closer to the dam. The orange boom with its heavy steel cable would ensnare his propeller if he tried to cross it. He also realized that the snails might be destroyed or eaten by large bass and carp before they could reach the 300-yard distance to the dam. The fish would die from eating them, but he had to get the snails closer.

The video tape blinked as if it had been edited, then came back on. This time it was Moori sitting, dressed in a black robe and with the black flag in his left hand. He pointed upwards and praised that he would breach the heavy gate and fence at the entrance to the dam. He made his official jihad declaration of sacrifice.

"At two-fifty in the afternoon, I will drive fast and speed along the earthen top of the 200-foot high dam. Then I will plunge into the lake at two-fifty-three near the massive concrete flood gates. At two-fifty-five, the flood gates will open automatically, and my weapon shall begin to do its work. The snails and shrimp eggs will spill into the water where the truck crashed and will travel through the gates and on towards Atlanta. I plan to die as a martyr with this bold stroke. I ask of my ISIS brothers that my actions will redeem my wife and daughter's transgressions," Moori said on the video.

Stunned by this brilliant strategy, Brian paused the video player for a while. He rubbed the back of his neck like a student who had studied all night at a library desk. Then he continued to see what else was on the tape. It was Moori, dressed in a dress shirt and slacks, looking completely dejected. It was filmed on a later date. The tape showed Moori with his head down in shame.

"The Americans have constructed a concrete barrier to the service road that ran along the top of the dam. The truck I acquired will not be able to crash through. I must try the water approach. I need to get past that orange boom," said Moori on the video.

The video tape blinked and a new section began with Moori in a much happier mood.

"I have studied the other way and deemed it crucial to destroy the dam. If the dam's release gates were to be disabled by attacking the engineering station and killing the technicians, the dam would begin to become overloaded with the stress of tons and tons of excess lake water. Many dams have failed this way, causing cracks in the concrete which later fail or even result in a catastrophic collapse. If I do this and release the scaegrots at the same time, the authorities wouldn't dare open the flood gates. Either way, the destruction would be devastating. Hurricane season is approaching and with it many storms that would inundate the lake basin with rain water. ISIS would have its victory, and terror and misery would be my great triumph," Moori said on the video.

Brian felt confused and guilty. He had killed an extremist fighter who was on a special mission. The attack was a great one, which would bring much destruction immediately or over several years. However, with Moori dead, Brian realized that this attack was now to become his destiny. He would pick up where Moori left off. He needed to get to the dam and see for himself where the orange boom could be bypassed.

Brian made his way back upstairs. He went to the kitchen and grabbed some pita bread and poured himself some water to drink. He then went back to the recliner to eat and think. The television was still on the foreign station. He changed the channel and watched the news while at the same time he searched for more information on the stolen cellphone about how many dams have failed due to excessive rainfall. He sat upright when he saw the news station report its next big story. A story he believed that only providence would have given him.

The meteorologist on the TV set showed the progress of Isaac, now a Category 2 storm, coming that way. He displayed a large red swirl on the map which simulated the hurricane and the red path of destruction it would likely take. The destination was the Georgia coastline and inland.

"Either way, you are all going to be covered in red—my red," Brian said.

CHAPTER 45

Old Lessons Learned

In the governor's office, a heavy, wooden paneled door creaked open, and an aide to Gov. Nodell stuck his head inside and politely mentioned that the President was on the secure line for him.

Nodell, the state attorney, and other legal aides stopped talking. All eyes became fixated on the dark blue phone with a flashing red notification light. Silence filled the room.

"Hello, Mr. President. It is so good of you to call. How can I help you?"

"You know damn well why I'm calling, governor. Now cut this bullshit about the dam and release it back to the Corps of Engineers. Senators from Alabama and Florida are screaming mad and want your head on a stick. Public opinion thinks your nuts, and my generals are itching to kick your guys back into the Stone Age," said the President on the other end of the receiver.

"Mr. President," Nodell started the conversation in a low voice after a hard clearing of his throat. "Sir, with all due respect to our wonderful and blessed Union, it was my decision to seize the Buford Dam and bring the sister states of Alabama and Florida back to the negotiation table over our differences in water needs. We had the foresight to plan for our water resources."

"With government funding!" said the President.

"In two days, the dam will be returned to you. We are now scheduled to begin a more productive negotiation settlement tomorrow. The "Water Wars" will come to a peaceful solution. I will then resign as governor after everything is settled. Please, sir. I pray that you will make no attempt to recapture the dam, or the course of history will change against you. As we speak, our press officers and legal teams are informing the national media of this agreement. I truly hope you will see the wisdom in it and give me two days."

"Do you have any idea that there is a hurricane headed your way?" asked the President.

"All the more reason for everyone to participate quickly, Mr. President. I bid you good day, sir."

And with that, Nodell hung up the phone.

The whole office was absolutely quiet. Staff members and officers for the governor felt uneasy and began to squirm in their seats. Some of the legal department personnel in the room began looking at their smart phones for any bits of news from the media.

"Ladies and gentlemen, may I have all of your attention, please. I want my legacy for the State of Georgia to be one that is ready for the future. I do not intend for it to be squabbling over small aquatic life in the Chattahoochee River. I want commerce to thrive in the South. I want Alabama and Florida to enjoy the gifts of water as we do. If any of you wish to leave and not be a part of this historic moment, you have my permission. There will be no repercussions if you decide to do so," said Nodell.

There was a silent pause for a moment, but no one left the room.

"I remind you all of what my grandfather did for Georgia in the railroad industry. Atlanta is the key hub for all of the South. He also said these fine words: 'In a place where everyone drinks and uses the same water from the creek, it is better to be up stream.' Be vigilant, folks. Our state laws give me the emergency powers to do what I am doing as long as Washington is informed. Well, by God, I think they just got notice," laughed Nodell as he tapped the desk and looked over to the state attorney for approval.

The state's senior lawyer nodded a positive nod and winked back at the governor.

CHAPTER 46

The Wolf Sees Its Shadow

The next morning was met with the four teenagers on the pontoon boat with the *Wolf*. Michael wanted everyone to understand how the submarine worked from top to bottom. He surmised with Steve that if all knew how the *Wolf* worked, then new and fresh ideas might bloom. The group proceeded out of their cove and headed towards the dam. Steve reminded his older brother that there was another tub of the C02 scrubber placed inside the sub.

After about a half-hour of cruising on the lake avoiding the regular vacationing boaters, the pontoon boat moved into a secluded cove. The anchor was dropped from the stern end of the boat when the motor stopped. The blue tarp and wood slats were removed, and the *Wolf* was lowered into the water.

Steve and Elizabeth piloted the sub this time. Steve was a bit nervous, for it was Elizabeth's turn to drive. The lowering ropes were removed from the triangle hooks. Elizabeth looked up and smiled at Jack, and Michael told her she would do fine.

"What about me?" asked Steve.

Everyone laughed at Steve's imitation of a little puppy in the window routine. His hands were up like a puppy begging for scraps.

In a few minutes, the sub glided out from the pontoon boat. The conning tower was then closed, and Elizabeth began her dive. She worked the valves perfectly as the sub moved forward. She rolled the box seat forward and changed the trim of the *Wolf* to go nose first. Steve was very impressed by his cousin as she deftly handled the sub.

Steve said nothing as he closed his eyes and crossed himself. The inside was silent as the hissing bubbles escaped from the lifting pontoons as they slowly filled with cold lake water.

"Deck is awash," Elizabeth said as she peered through the periscope.

"Where did you learn that phrase?"

"Oh, I've seen a war movie or two," Elizabeth said.

In a few seconds, the *Wolf* was underwater. Elizabeth rolled the seat backwards with Steve's help to trim the sub. Both then searched the inside of the sub for any leaks. To Steve's relief, none were found.

"Oh, relax, you big baby. We're coming up in a minute," Elizabeth said.

"Oh, I wasn't scared, just excited about your first command."

Elizabeth turned her head towards Steve's back and stuck out her tongue. The two laughed, and Steve relaxed.

Suddenly, the depth finder shrieked an alarm. A red light on the upper right corner of the screen was followed by a buzzer which sounded on the little, black fish-finder box. Like an angry bumblebee inside a Chinese take-home box, the buzzing alarm's vibration was unmistakable. The *Wolf* was too close to the bottom—or something worse.

"What happened?" Steve asked.

"I don't know. I'm stopping forward thrust and adding air to the pontoons so we can get out of here," Elizabeth said.

The two froze in panic as they heard scratching noises on the outside of the *Wolf's* hull. Like a large claw grinding its way across the forward right side of the sub, the sounds truly terrified Elizabeth and Steve.

The *Wolf* stopped moving, as if held in place by some massive creature.

"I'm adding more air to the pontoons. We have got to climb up and get away from this thing," Elizabeth said.

"This isn't fun anymore," Steve said.

The *Wolf* started to climb, but it was quickly ensnared again by some immense claw. Elizabeth and Steve heard more scratching noises from outside the hull. This time a small moan was heard like a large door was being opened slowly after having been shut for years.

"What was that?" asked Steve.

"Whatever has got us is not happy we bumped into it," Elizabeth said.

Up on the surface, Michael leaned over the railings of the pontoon boat. Jack went to the wheel to help start the motor and steer if needed. What they saw was where the *Wolf* was supposed to be, yet all they could see was a whole bunch of bubbles rising to the surface.

"She's blowing too much air from the tanks. Why is she doing that? Something's wrong," Michael said.

The dark green waters on the surface swirled and danced as if something below was swimming in circles. Bubbles rose to the top and popped and hissed as the released compressed air broke the surface.

"They're in trouble," Jack said.

"Yeah, but how can we help them? Maybe I should dive in and see. Give me that mask," Michael said.

Michael quickly donned the swimming mask, pulled off his shoes and his blue jeans, and jumped into the cold dark water.

"Hey, you'll need this," Jack said as he threw a flashlight over to Michael.

Michael caught it and gave a thumbs-up sign. He then went below the water. Fearful that he might be diving into the Wolf's propeller, Michael swam around the supposed location.

After a minute of swimming, he had to return to the surface to get another breath of air. The water was colder than normal in the cove. Perhaps the sun didn't have enough time to heat the water, or perhaps there was some underwater spring that fed a colder current into the lake. Whatever it was, it sapped the strength out of Michael's legs. Caution began to fill his mind as he remembered that many people have succumbed to cold water and have drowned.

"You okay?" asked Jack.

Another thumbs-up sign and Michael went back down. This time he heard the bubbles and the whine of the sub's prop. The *Wolf* was fighting to set itself free. He also heard that unusual moan from the deep. The scratching noises unnerved him as well. He turned on the flashlight and pointed it in the direction of the noises.

The sub with its gray-painted hull was difficult to make out at first, but when Michael saw the *Wolf's* sigil on the conning tower, he knew he had found her. His submarine was in trouble, for it appeared that she has been captured by a green, slimy underwater monster.

Michael discovered that the *Wolf* was tangled in a large, underwater tree. The cold water had preserved the tree since the lake was created by building the Buford Dam in 1956. The light from the flashlight illuminated the danger. A large tree limb was above the sub and blocked Elizabeth's attempts from rising. He swam deeper and tapped on the hull three times with the flashlight.

"It's Michael," Steve said.

Elizabeth nodded in approval and turned to hug Steve with relief.

Michael rose to the surface and yelled to Jack to get the boat running and move closer to his location. He also demanded for one of the winch ropes to be thrown to him. Jack quickly obliged.

"They're stuck in an old tree. We have to pull the sub backwards. I'm going to go down and tie the rope to the rear lifting hook. When I come back up, put the pontoon boat in reverse and tow the *Wolf* backwards," Michael said.

Jack acknowledged and made his preparations to assist. The pontoon boat was responsive and moved across the water as it should. The winch rope was paid out from the swing set crane and tossed to Michael.

Michel grabbed the rope and dove under. He tapped on the sub's hull once again and knocked to the tune of "Shave and a Haircut."

Inside the *Wolf*, Elizabeth and Steve laughed as they recognized that classic knock. Steve reached down and tapped with a wrench on the sub wall the two knocks in response.

Michael, holding his breath as best he could, finished tying the rope to the sub and rose to the surface. When he made it to the top, he told Jack to start his tow.

The pontoon boat's engine churned deep as the motor pulled through the water. Michael gave another thumbs-up sign.

"We're doing it," Jack said.

The very next moment, with its diving pontoons full of air, the *Wolf* broke free from the massive limb and, like a cork, quickly rose to the surface. The tow rope fell loose onto the propeller that was still turning, but the fan screen used to keep weeds from fouling the prop did its job. Michael quickly swam over to make sure the rope didn't do any damage.

Jack eased back on the boat motor in reverse and slowly brought the pontoon boat over in position to retrieve the sub.

Michael smacked the hull two times with his hand as if spanking the *Wolf* for misbehaving. In a very special moment, Michael got quiet and thought to himself that he was proud of his creation. It was a bond that inventor and creation shared.

"You are a good girl," he said to the *Wolf*.

A commotion was then heard from within the sub. A minute later, the conning tower opened and Steve was the first to stand up and ask what happened. Elizabeth sat still inside the sub to maintain balance and turned off everything inside that drew power from the batteries.

"You guys ran into an old tree. The branches and limbs were holding you down. Jack and I pulled you out," Michael said.

Elizabeth looked back to the pontoon boat and gave a big smile to Jack.

With the excitement over, the group hauled the *Wolf* out of the water and started efforts to head back home. All were proud of how lucky things turned out, but they also realized an important truth. Diving into an area that was unknown was far too dangerous. Until they could perfect the sonar fish-finder to see underwater obstacles, they all agreed it was taboo.

Michael motored carefully out of the cove and turned the wheel towards Hall Harbor. In the distance was one of the rental pontoon boats from the marina. A dark figure with a black beard, stocking cap, and binoculars was behind the wheel and had been watching the events that unfolded in the cove. The rental boat wasn't moving. It just stopped in the channel and rocked back and forth with the lake's waves.

"Hey, guys, that creepy dude has been watching us," Michael said.

Jack and Steve looked at the stranger while Elizabeth looked down and away. Michael slowly brought the boat up to speed and passed the intruding houseboat as the stranger looked on.

Elizabeth slowly looked up to see what the commotion was all about. She gazed out towards the direction of the other boat. When she focused on the stranger, the man lowered his binoculars and their eyes met. She froze in her seat with fear as she saw his face. His eyes were beady, dark specks that glowed in the shadow of the Bimini umbrella on the rental. What happened in a few seconds seemed like hours to Elizabeth. The stare was so frightening to her that she shuddered. Jack looked back and noticed her uneasiness.

"You okay?" he asked.

"I just saw evil, Jack. Whoever that man was, he was pure evil."

The pontoon boat that the group was on made another course change and headed home. The *Wolf* was covered in its familiar blue tarp and strapped down for the bumpy ride as Michael increased the throttle. The boat picked up speed as it sped away.

From the other boat, still adrift in the channel of the lake, a laugh came across the stranger's lips. He put the binoculars down onto the console panel and started up the motor of the rental boat. Brian stalked his prey from a distance.

"Perfect for my needs to get under the boom," Brian said.

CHAPTER 47

Love Can Be Blind

"Elizabeth, won't you come with us? I'm taking the boys to the racetrack to show them a new Lotus sports car I'm thinking about buying. We'll be back around lunch," asked Mike Cotter as the boys climbed in the car.

Elizabeth shook her head, stretched, and yawned. Her fuzzy pink bathrobe picked up a few pine straws along the sidewalk.

"No, sir. I'm not feeling well today. Girl stuff," she answered.

A few minutes later, Mr. Cotter's black sedan sped off and was gone.

When she knew they were gone, Elizabeth pulled off her robe, revealing that she had shorts and a t-shirt underneath. A quick text message appeared on her phone. It was from Jack. He asked if it was all clear; Elizabeth answered his text.

From the lake, Elizabeth heard a loud whistle. It was Jack, who had come out from the brush. He waved his arms to say hello.

Elizabeth blushed and then waved back to Jack. She slid her feet into some flip flops and started downhill.

Jack wore a navy blue baseball cap, t-shirt, and a pair of shorts. He pulled a light blue, foldable cart, normally used by boaters to get from auto to dock, loaded with three heavy bags of sand. He met Elizabeth at the boat house.

The two smiled with excitement like two people who had just met for the first time on a date. She brushed back her hair behind her ears. Jack pulled up his shorts to fit better around his waist.

"They'll be gone for four hours at least," Elizabeth said.

"Great! Help me get these sand bags on board."

The two loaded up the pontoon boat. Elizabeth started the engine while

Jack untied the lines.

The pontoon boat slowly backed out from the boat house. Jack proceeded to wrap a blue tarp over the *Wolf* to hide it from onlookers as they made their way out into the open waters of the lake.

As the sun glistened on the water, the pontoon boat headed for the large marina to the left.

Known to all who enjoy the lake, Hall Harbor was a haven for all the big houseboats and sailboats. Strategically positioned, one could be at the dam and watch a beautiful sunset within thirty minutes.

"I'm glad we are together today, Elizabeth. You are much sweeter than Michael," Jack said shyly.

"I like you, too."

The two rubbed shoulders in an awkward show of affection as the pontoon boat continued its course.

"Let's drop anchor here," Jack said.

"What are we going to do?"

"I'm going to be very careful, but I want to launch my own torpedo. I never did it yesterday, and, well, it kind of pissed me off," Jack said defiantly.

"No, Jack. You don't have permission from Michael. Plus it takes two people to make the *Wolf* work," she protested.

"I've got it all figured out. The sandbags will be the weight of another person. You lower me down, and I'll unhook the ropes and close the hatch. Then I will go under and move forward several yards. I'll fire my torpedo at something, and you can come and pick me up. We'll be back at the boat house in two hours."

Sadly, Elizabeth agreed and slowed the motor to a stop. She then headed to the stern and dropped the spade-like Danforth anchor over the starboard side.

The pontoons on the boat chopped side to side like a see saw as the wakes of the boats coming and going from Hall Harbor created the manmade sea state.

Jack opened the sub's hatch. A red-winged wasp fluttered from the tarp, disturbed from its hiding place. Jack bravely swatted the wasp down using his baseball cap.

"Die, you bastard!" Jack yelled with a touch of fear and excitement mixed in his emotions.

"My brave Jackson, but I don't like that language you used." Elizabeth said with a smile and a laugh.

"I think I remember the boys saying you used some colorful word yourself when you got attacked by wasps." He then added, "He must have dropped down from the roof of the boat house."

The two laughed as the unusual tension about what they were

attempting subsided.

The sub was raised slightly to allow the slats to be removed. Then it was lowered partially to allow Jack to heave the sand bags into the boat. He then checked all the things that Michael would always do before a launch.

"The *Wolf* is ready," Jack said as he climbed into the sub.

Elizabeth, at the winch, cranked slowly downwards, knowing deep down inside that this was wrong. She wanted Jack to have his wish, but she did not know any other way.

Jack knew this was his moment. He looked up at Elizabeth and gave a silly salute.

"Today, the *Wolf* will show it has teeth," he said.

He then proceeded to unhook the ropes that had lowered the sub into the water.

Jack throttled the electric motor to move the sub forward, waved goodbye, and closed the hatch.

Elizabeth sat and watched the *Wolf* begin to slowly submerge and start towards the marina. Her stomach turned in knots with guilt and made her seasick as the pontoon boat jostled in the waves.

The submarine, finally submerged, disappeared into the diamond-like reflections from the sun.

"Please be careful," she whispered.

CHAPTER 48

I'm in Charge, I Think?

Carl enjoyed his new position. His job that day was to monitor the lake for suspicious activity from his boat so as to not draw attention from the ones who didn't want to be seen.

The boat's radio was set on channel 16, which was the station everyone paid attention to. The usual chatter was being exchanged from boat captain to boat captain. Calls for a raft up or meeting at a favorite cove to swim or sunbathe were the norm.

Carl even wore his lucky red Hawaiian shirt just to play the unsuspecting part. Using government-issued binoculars, he surveyed the lake for anything.

He slowed his boat down to inspect his favorite anchoring spot, Wild Man's Cove. As the boat slowed, Carl spotted two speed boats lashed together. Some people were in the water around the back end of the boats.

A pair of tanned female arms reached up and grabbed the speed boat's swim ladder. The woman climbing up the ladder, topless and very fit for her age, boarded one of the boats and began to dry off.

"Now that's what I'm talking about," Carl said as he peered through the binoculars.

An unshaved grin emerged on Carl's face as he continued to invade her privacy. He watched every towel stroke and body part rubbed. However, Carl didn't notice that someone else had climbed aboard the anchored boat.

A very buff man in his thirties wearing black swim trunks waved angrily and caught Carl's attention. Carl suddenly realized he'd been caught peeking. The man moved the topless woman out of sight and covered her with a large towel. He then reached down and picked up a long, black-looking object.

"Shit, he's got a gun!" Carl said as he quickly put down the binoculars and reached for the steering wheel and throttle.

Carl's boat sprung to life as it made a sharp right turn and headed back out to the lake.

Carl took one last peek behind him. He watched as another woman climbed out of the water. The first woman stood up to help.

"You pervert!" screamed the man over the boat's radio on channel 16.

"Anybody listening on this station, there's a boat with a fat jerk wearing a red Hawaiian shirt. I caught him watching us with binoculars while we were swimming," the irate man cautioned.

"Clear this station and use a different channel," said a Coast Guard Auxiliary person over the channel.

"Channel 16 is for monitoring," continued the retired female dispatcher.

As a volunteer, she and her colleagues monitored 16 for emergencies and towing requests.

Carl was far enough away to unbutton his shirt and take it off. He placed the shirt in the cockpit seat behind him; he wiped the sweat from his forehead with one of his hands.

"Thank you, lucky shirt. That was close," he laughed to himself.

Carl then took a sip of his beer and turned the boat's heading 180 degrees and went back to the marina.

"Maybe Joyce would like to come by and get lucky like me?"

Just as Carl's boat completed his new course change, the lake winds shifted and blew the red Hawaiian shirt out of the cockpit seat and into the lake. It sank fast in the churned-up waters from his boat; Carl lost sight of his lucky shirt as he sped ahead.

"Damn," he muttered as he looked on.

CHAPTER 49

The Wolf and Her First Kill

"Almost there," Jack said quietly as he viewed through the sub's periscope.

The *Wolf* was two feet under the water and moving on a straight course towards the entrance of the marina. The whirl of the propeller was great to listen to while under water. The voltage meter displayed on the front console indicated that all three batteries for the sub were still very well-charged.

Like a lion approaching a herd of gazelles under the cover of tall grass, the *Wolf* crept closer.

Jack could hear the whine of high-speed propellers from several distant speed boats which zoomed in and around the harbor entrance. He could even hear the buzzing sound of jet skis as they zoomed like the wasps in the Cotters' boat house. It was a beautiful day, and everyone with a boat wanted to enjoy it.

Jack sweated profusely from the dampness inside of the submarine. He was filled with excitement. His baseball cap was turned backwards like the submarine skippers did as they peered through their periscopes. Jack always did his best to copy such old, quirky things. Michael and Steve were great history buffs, and Jack wanted them to know he was an equal. He also remembered the old war films he would watch at the Cotters' house when he got to sleep over.

"I'm going to be so excited if this works. I'll have to get several more of these torpedoes," he said to himself.

He enjoyed every minute at the periscope. Then Jack began to hear a deep churning sound, something in the distance which sounded like an old dishwasher machine during its soak cycle. A slow and constant *whoosh-*

whoosh-whoosh could be heard. The sound grew louder as Jack vainly tried to see what was coming out of the harbor's entrance.

Then he saw her. It was a massive houseboat. Built on an old barge, the giant vessel moved like a slow elephant. Some houseboat giants were overloaded with Jacuzzi hot tubs, pianos, marbled tile flooring, and even a fully stocked wine cellar. The boat Jack saw through his periscope must have had it all. The barge moved painfully slow as the underpowered engine struggled under its intense mass to move through the water.

The houseboat's image quickly filled the periscope's view screen as it passed abreast of the *Wolf*. The name stenciled on the side of the pleasure craft was *Smooth Ride*.

With a distance of about 60 to 65 yards, Jack suddenly realized that this was his target of opportunity.

Perfect. It's slow and big, so I can't miss. The people having that party on board wouldn't think a thing when the torpedo hits. The only evidence would be the red paintball splatter marking the hit. Oh, I hope Elizabeth is watching and recording this, Jack thought to himself.

Meanwhile, Elizabeth followed Jack's instructions and released another one of Steve and Michael's black camera boats to record the torpedo hit. The small remote-control boat motored off towards the *Wolf*'s last known position. She then toggled the camera switch on and steered the little craft to a forward-looking position to video the torpedo exploding red paint on the side of the boat.

The submarine was brought to a stop. Jack wanted the houseboat to cross his front. He carefully waited and grasped the pulling wire that activated the torpedo's electric motor.

"Wait. Wait. Steady. Steady," droned Jack out loud.

He guessed that the large target was probably doing three knots to avoid wake issues with the harbor's rules, and his torpedo would need to be released in about ten seconds to intercept.

"Tube one, fire!" he bellowed.

With that, Jack pulled the wire lanyard and started the underwater missile on its one-time painting adventure.

The torpedo's powerful, little, counter-rotating propellers kept it straight and true as it maintained a straight course towards the barge. Only a faint trail of bubbles followed in its wake.

"There it goes. Come on, my son. Come on, my son," grinned Jack as he quoted Peter O'Toole's adventures with a German torpedo in the movie *Murphy's War*.

Through the periscope, Jack saw the torpedo hit. Red paint splattered across the lower hull of the houseboat. A perfect hit for the first kill.

"He did it!" cried Elizabeth.

She watched with binoculars on the distant pontoon boat. In her excitement, the remote-control box fell off her lap onto the pontoon deck. It was an accident soon to be forgotten as the next events unfolded.

Jack shouted with joy inside the sub as he began the process to return to the surface. He reached for the pressure valves and started the turns.

Then, suddenly, he heard a different noise coming from the underwater sounds of the houseboat. A grinding sound like metal on metal.

Jack looked back up and peered through the periscope as the sub was just under the surface. What he saw horrified him.

The paint torpedo had hit its mark and spewed red paint on the hull, but the torpedo floated alongside the barge and did not sink. Worse still, by horrible luck, the torpedo's frame made its way to the back of the houseboat. It was then sucked underneath and lodged itself in the prop's shaft and mounting arm of the boat's slow-turning propeller.

The added strain to the overtaxed motor of the houseboat was too much for the engine to bear. The increased friction caused the motor to overheat and catch fire. The barge began to shudder and lost more power.

The boat's command panel flashed warning red lights which indicated trouble. The captain went below to see what had happened with his engine. A fire alarm klaxon sounded throughout the boat as sensors in the engine compartment recognized an engine fire. Quickly, the captain went to get a fire extinguisher. He left his wife on the top observation deck to man the helm.

Below, amidst the inebriated party guests, the captain opened the engine room door. He was met by a huge fireball emerging as fresh oxygen was provided by opening the sealed compartment. This action burned his face and hands. Unfazed, the captain released all of the fire extinguisher's contents. In a white, powdery blast and haze, the fire seemed to be snuffed out. The partiers nearby applauded and toasted the captain's brave heroics. Then the revelers proceeded back to the bar to refill their glasses.

The flames soon returned. The fire ignited the wood paneling nearby and forced the dumbfounded captain to frantically search for another extinguisher. Everyone started to scream in panic. The captain then realized that he had made some serious flaws in judgment. He had too many people on board, and he had not replaced the other fire extinguisher which he had used when the outdoor grill had started a grease fire. Finally, he realized he had no one sober enough to help him.

Meanwhile, Jack had not surfaced. He sadly watched what he had done, but he knew that he would be in serious trouble if he rose up now. With his hand, he pushed the electric motor throttle into reverse to back away slowly beneath the waves.

Elizabeth brought up the anchor with a sense of panic. She needed to get Jack and the *Wolf* out of there as soon as possible.

Below, in the engine room of the doomed ship, the flames continued to spread. The guests began to cry and started moving to the front of the boat. Some of the guests crossed themselves and prayed for rescue.

Above, the wife tried her best to turn the steering wheel of the boat towards a nearby beach. She also wanted to avoid a rusted, metal shallow water marker. About the size of a corner post for cattle fences and barbed wire, this post had been firmly planted by the Corps years ago and was easily marked for day or night cruising and was easily avoidable. However, the flames had already compromised the hydraulic steering for the vessel, and the houseboat was on a collision course. Within a minute, the boat ran over the marker. Since the lake was at full pool, the shallow draft of the *Smooth Ride* carried her over the sand reef below the waves. The metal post bent with the heavy mass of the ship, but it dragged and scraped the bottom of the hull and keel like someone's fingernails running across a chalk board. If there were any large rust spots below, that post would surely find its mark and puncture a gash, letting in lake water. When the barge finally cleared the post, the rudder took the last hit. The post bent the rudder slightly to the left, causing the *Smooth Ride* to steer away from the beach. Heading out to the middle of the lake was the worst thing possible, and it was definitely not what the captain wanted.

Huge, billowy clouds of black, burning smoke filled the insides of this giant pleasure craft and trailed out the back end of the tragedy-ridden vessel. The only safe place for the passengers was topside on the observation deck.

Life vests and a life ring were gathered and passed out as the families and friends prepared for the worse. Some of the men gave their vests to other people when it was discovered there were not enough to go around. Carried by her father, a young girl named Stephanie, who had been wheelchair-bound since birth, was brought upstairs to keep her in the fresh air. The wheelchair that been Stephanie's only means of transportation remained below. Fitted with a life jacket, she began to cry uncontrollably in her father's arms.

"Look!" cried a passenger as he pointed off in the distance about 65 yards out to the right of the boat.

The gray periscope of the *Wolf* appeared in the distance, followed by propeller splashes, and finally the back end of the sub breached the surface. Jack was in reverse, but he forgot to trim the balance of the submarine with the rolling seat. The back end came up to the surface, exposing the *Wolf* completely. The passengers and captain all looked in disbelief that their pleasure cruise had been attacked by a submarine.

"What the hell is that thing?" asked another.

"Mayday! Mayday! Mayday! This is the houseboat *Smooth Ride* just outside the harbor entrance of Hall Harbor. We have been attacked by a submarine off our starboard quarter. I am declaring a Mayday. We have an engine room fire out of control. I have twenty-two people on board. I say again: two-two souls on board. One is handicapped. Steering non-responsive, smoke and fire increasing, and I believe the hull has been punctured. Request all aid! Over," cried the captain into the handheld walkie-talkie on channel 16.

"*Smooth Ride*, this is the Coast Guard Auxiliary Station. We have received your Mayday, and you said you were attacked? By a submarine? We have dispatched the commercial tow boat company to assist you," came a reply from the handset.

Within seconds, the call went out for the assist. However, the commercial tow boat company's base was on the other side of the lake. Transmissions were sometimes sketchy due to the distance and length of the lake. Spectators from other boats and on shore could hear on their radios the attempts by the Coast Guard Auxiliary to contact the tow boat company. It was confused and garbled, resulting in neither one understanding the other.

There was that day a 33-foot sailboat named *Ladybug* that was in the halfway spot of the two groups trying to communicate with each other. Close to a reef called Gilligan's Reef and a near a small island, the sailboat's captain, along with his wife who was sunbathing upfront, and his mother who was enjoying her second scotch in the cockpit, picked up his hand radio and relayed the messages for both parties. His actions quickly helped get things started as others joined in to help. There was almost too much radio traffic, and the USCGA had to ask for everyone to clear channel 16.

From the harbor, a small flotilla of speed boats and other vessels left to offer assistance. One large motor boat, its captain bare-chested with dark sunglasses, raced to the doomed barge and deliberately rammed the burning ship on the left bow. It was a heavy hit which caused the passengers on board to be alarmed, but the effect was well worth it. The *Smooth Ride's* course was redirected back towards the sandy beach some 200 yards away.

Another boat rode up alongside and tossed three life vests to the passengers. One of the vests strayed and landed in the flames and burned. Other people tried to help with their boats as well. Some offered to take away any passengers who wanted to jump ship. One of the boys wanted to jump onto the speedboat, but the lake was way too choppy by then and the boy fell into the water. A boat that followed the *Smooth Ride* picked up the boy.

There was even a group of fraternity brothers who had celebrated the night before at the marina. They came up and offered their assistance to the doomed ship. One of the college boys even held up a precious, left-over six-pack of cold beer to offer to the passengers.

"Are you fricking kidding me!" yelled the captain of the *Smooth Ride.*

Yet still, the danger was real. The barge was headed to the beach. The captain ordered everyone to slide down the swim slide when the boat landed onshore. He told two of the men to go first and then assist others as they came down the deck-mounted slide.

The barge made it to the sandy beach and slowed to a gentle stop. No longer forced out the rear of the boat by the winds of moving forward, the huge clouds of black smoke and flames now raced forward to attack the survivors.

"Everybody, go, go!" yelled the captain.

Like an airplane evacuation down inflated chutes, everyone slid down the slide and walked ashore. The father carried his daughter down the slide, and he thanked all who had helped.

The captain helped his wife slide down. He quickly looked around and asked if everyone had left. Then he abandoned the *Smooth Ride* as she began to burn uncontrollably.

Everybody was safe.

The boats who had offered assistance came up and either anchored or beached their craft nearby to offer first aid and support. A fire truck approached in the distance. In a short span of time, there were firemen and paramedics who ran to the water's edge and treated the survivors. A pine tree close by caught fire, and a fire hose was brought forward and quickly doused the flames.

Above the chaos, the rotor sounds of a news helicopter could be heard as it videoed the events that unfolded below. The helicopter was from one of the three big stations that covered metro Atlanta. Once they filmed the events that unfolded below and reported the story, it was time to head back to base and refuel.

"Where is that bastard? Where is he? Does anybody see that submarine?" asked the captain.

Some of the responders pointed in the general direction of the last whereabouts of the sub.

A DNR patrol boat arrived at the scene. The green-clad officers came ashore to offer assistance.

"Officers! Good. There is a submarine out there that attacked my boat. I want that boat caught. They did this!" cried the captain as he gestured with his arms and pointed to the burned hulk of the *Smooth Ride* and to the survivors.

"A submarine? Here on Lake Lanier? What did it look like?" asked one of the officers.

"Gray with a conning tower and a black periscope," said one of the survivors.

"The sub was three meters long. Probably an electric boat," answered the father as he held Stephanie in his arms. The wheelchair had burned up with the boat.

"Hey, I got something on my cellphone. It is a news story about the submarine in the lake. There's even a picture of the submarine—must have been from that news copter above," said someone from the passengers.

Silence hushed all that were involved in the conversation. One of the officers looked at the father and Stephanie with his head cocked like a canine hearing a command from his master but not understanding the words.

"How come you know so much about submarines?" asked the officer.

"What? I did time in the Navy on antisubmarine duty in the Mediterranean. The Russians have built hundreds of those little pocket subs and sold them to every known terrorist in the region. Hell, the South American drug cartels use them to slip past the Coast Guard," said the father.

Quickly, the officers returned to their patrol boat and sped away as they flashed their blue lights. They proceeded to where the civilians had pointed to the possible location.

CHAPTER 50

What Did We Do?

Elizabeth cried when she cranked up the *Wolf* into its hauled-up position on the pontoon boat. Jack quickly placed the two boards underneath to support the sub, and then he brought it down to rest on the deck. Jack then covered the sub with the blue tarp. Elizabeth came over and hugged and kissed Jack sweetly on his cheek—a kiss that almost touched his lips. It was at that moment that Jack felt something in his gut about Elizabeth. He had always heard everybody talk about butterflies in their stomachs; now he knew it was real.

"We need to get going," Jack said.

The pontoon boat picked up speed and headed back to the boat house. The two patrol boats swept back and forth and searched for any sign of the submarine.

Carl was finally close by after he had heard the emergency calls on 16 as well as on the DNR frequency. He recognized his buddy Thomas was on boat number 4. He picked up the radio, and he hailed Thomas to pull over for a second.

Carl's boat and patrol boat number 4 pulled up beside each other as the skippers talked. Thomas' partner scanned the nearby coves with binoculars. With all the civilian rescue craft in the area, it was difficult to observe.

"There! That pontoon boat leaving the scene. Just passed the little lighthouse. It has something hidden under a blue tarp. Let's go," ordered the partner.

Instantly, the DNR patrol boat's twin 220 Mercury engines kicked in full throttle in pursuit. This sudden action caused Carl's boat to rock in the severe chop. Thomas' partner pulled out the boat's automatic assault rifle from a foot locker on the deck.

"DNR Patrol 4 in pursuit of unknown craft carrying concealed cargo. May be our sub," radioed Thomas.

"Roger. Proceed with extreme caution. Carl is your back-up until patrols 2 and 3 arrive," answered back the dispatcher.

In under four minutes, patrol 4 caught up with the pontoon boat. Thomas' partner trained his assault rifle on the target while Thomas got on the bullhorn.

"Unknown pontoon boat. This is the Department of Natural Resources. Heave to and prepare to be boarded," he ordered.

Elizabeth and Jack were about 75 yards away from the boat house when she throttled back the engine. The pontoon boat slowed then finally stopped.

Both young adults raised their hands in surrender.

The DNR craft slowed and prepared to grapple and lash on to the boat. The air was tense with fear as the two boats were lashed to each other.

Carl slowly approached in his boat about 200 yards astern, but then he noticed something in the water and brought his boat to a stop. With a pole, he fished out of the lake a little remote-controlled boat that had a camera. It was black and motorized just like the other one he had caught when he was on the date with Joyce.

"Well, son of a bitch! Look what I caught. Wait until Bill sees this," he crowed.

Elizabeth's cellphone rang on the dashboard of the cockpit. With her hands still raised, she looked down to see who was calling her.

"Who is it?" Jack whispered.

"It's my uncle."

"Be quiet!" ordered Thomas as he boarded the boat.

The DNR officer instructed the two to sit on the gray floor rug of the pontoon boat. Thomas then took controls of the captured craft and drove the pontoon boat to a sandy spot and beached. The pontoon boat was parked very close to where the Cotters lived. The dock was only a hundred yards away. The other officer followed in the patrol boat and did the same.

"We're screwed," mumbled Jack.

"Ya think?" replied Elizabeth.

CHAPTER 51

The Mole and the Rat

Deep inside one of the Cabinet rooms for the governor was a small office. Originally a file room, it had been converted into an office for the usual flock of interns from several local colleges. That night, the office was empty and no one was on the phone.

One of Nodell's trusted officers, Desmond Maulwurf, who had been at Nodell's side all day, picked up the handset and dialed from memory a number he had dialed many times late at night.

"Hello, this is Tell," answered a female voice on the other end.

Telia Shire was the political reporter for a local television investigative news team. She had an unusual knack for acquiring the most sensitive information and gossip on all of Georgia's political leaders. Dressed in a grey skirt with a white blouse, the blonde, brown-eyed reporter was always ready to go to the street and get her latest story.

An unusual pinkish mole grew on the tip of her nose. She constantly had the makeup department cover her nose with some foundation or vanishing cream. A fashionable set of glasses hid her pair of dark brown eyes, but it was her two large front teeth that added to her distinctive features that she could not hide. Advised to have the teeth fixed and mole removed by her peers in the news industry, Tell, as was her nickname, had the imaginative look of a mouse, and she was deathly afraid of needles and dentists.

To some of the political figures that she had exposed or investigated, she was a genius in her reporting, but she was also called in private "The Rat."

"It's Thrasher," said Maulwurf.

The code name he used was the state bird, the Brown Thrasher.

Fittingly enough, his conversation thrashed the governor as he exposed the Guard's secret takeover of Lake Lanier's Buford Dam complex. He went on to mention that the Water Wars would soon be over, and that the President was involved in the secret negotiations. Then he quietly hung up the phone.

Telia couldn't believe her luck. The story being released in the morning about the house boat fire with casualties on Lake Lanier would tie in with the biggest scoop of the century. The State of Georgia had seized federal property, held the President at bay for two days while getting the negotiations done on the water problems with Alabama and Florida, and the governor's resignation was to follow. This was the jackpot story she had always dreamed about.

"As long as that hurricane stays away from the Georgia coast, the weather team will have to sit this one out. Because Tell is about to tell," she whispered to herself.

CHAPTER 52

Consequences

"What did they do officer?" asked Mike Cotter.

Standing on the lake shore, all the parties involved were there. Jack and Elizabeth were in handcuffs sitting down in the sand, their legs crossed.

Steve and Michael were angry at Jack, disappointed in Elizabeth, and sad that their *Wolf* was in the center of this tragic event.

The submarine was ingloriously uncovered as it rested on the deck of the pontoon boat. The *Wolf's* stenciled image was pointed upward on the conning tower as the hatch had been left open. It looked as if the sub was howling at the rising moon over the pine trees.

"Jack will be held in Juvenile Detention until his parents can be reached and bail set," the first deputy said.

"Elizabeth, though an accomplice to the incident, will be released under your watch. I think we can consider it a misdemeanor on her part. Probably some community service," the second deputy mentioned.

"Your boys built the sub but were not part of this tragedy. However, the submarine is your property and participated in this crime. It was Jack's torpedo that caused the damages. The sub must remain in your boat house, locked, and under surveillance. The Coast Guard will inspect it and deem whether or not it is seaworthy. Chances are it will have to be dismantled or destroyed, but until then, get yourself a good lawyer," said the first deputy.

A few minutes of silence past. Then the second deputy added even more news.

"The boat captain plans on suing you for damages to his boat. Luckily, no one was seriously injured. We have to go. Come along, Jack. We have to find your folks," finished the deputy.

"Wait," cried Elizabeth, as she rushed towards Jack and the officer helping him up.

She hugged Jack tightly and then she kissed him on the lips. The officer pulled the two apart and took Jack away.

No one else said a word as they turned and slowly walked back to the house.

Michael got on the pontoon boat and backed the boat off the beach and proceeded to the boat house. The conning tower hatch was still open.

Angry at the turn of events, he drove the boat into the slip forcefully. The pontoon boat banged and clashed hard into the dock, shaking all the contents inside the boat house and causing a few things to fall off the shelves. A plastic model of the aircraft carrier the *USS Constellation* fell and was lightly damaged when it hit the floor.

"Dammit! Damn it all to hell!" he cried to himself.

The *Wolf* was Michael's best creation—the coolest thing he had ever built—and now was ruined.

"It's all Jack's fault!" he yelled as he pounded a fist into one of the supporting posts.

"Michael, Dad wants you to finish up," Steve called down from the house.

"Okay, be right there," said Michael as he turned off the lights and left the conning tower hatch open to help air it out.

CHAPTER 53

I've Got an Idea

Brian was again half asleep in the recliner when the news story broke on channel 3 about a submarine striking a house boat with a torpedo. The story continued about some children who built the sub and fired the torpedo. This was the cause of a fire and resulting total loss of the boat. The story accompanied with a look-down video shot from a news helicopter showing a submarine moving away from the scene as the burning ship was beginning to flounder and beach.

Graphic video of the burned and injured survivors from Hall Harbor who had escaped the flames continued to be displayed behind the reporter.

"The submarine was a home project built by several youth in the lower western part of Hall County. Tragically, their talents went up in flames," commented the news anchor.

The story ended with the mention of an arrest of two suspects and the location of where the submarine and pontoon boat had been captured.

Brian sat upright in his chair. It was the boat he had spied on earlier. Excited by this news story, he got up and went back downstairs to the wall map of Lake Lanier. His fingers traced over the southwestern end of the lake, marking the cove where he had followed those kids. He then spotted the location where the boat burned. After that, he noticed on the map a marker showing a lighthouse. He remembered seeing that black and white lighthouse in the news video. Nearby was an old dock close to their house with a service road nearby. Brian studied the roads and the exact street where the kids' house was located.

"Ah, there you are," he said as his finger tapped the cove and the kids' lake home.

"That submarine will be the answer to do my last wish. Moori couldn’t go over the orange cable boom, but I can go under that cable. I shall atone Anya's sins, avenge my brothers in ISIS, and wreak havoc on a major city and three imperialistic states," he swore out loud with his right hand over his heart.

CHAPTER 54

Getting Closer

"Bill, I'm telling you, there's something fishy going on. Here's another one of those camera boats," Carl said as he tossed the wet model onto his desk.

Bill stood up, extremely upset. He moved some important paperwork out of the way of the lake water spilling from the RC boat. Next he picked it up and examined the craft.

"I'll have this sent to the FBI labs like the other one," Bill replied.

Carl nodded in agreement.

"I'm going to go over in my boat where that submarine came from, and I'll make sure it's there and stuff," Carl said as he walked out.

"You don't have a warrant to be on the property. Just stay loose and stay off shore," Bill responded.

CHAPTER 55

A Fresh Start

Elizabeth was just outside on the back patio, quietly crying and thinking about Jack as she sat on one of the Adirondack chairs. She held her head in her hands.

"Don't cry," whispered a sweet familiar voice.

Elizabeth sniffed and looked up. It was Jack. She jumped from her chair into his arms. A passionate kiss consumed them both.

"How did you get here? I thought they arrested you," she asked.

"My dad and your uncle posted bond until my hearing. Are you okay?" he asked between kisses.

"Come on. Let's go down to the dock and away from these lights," she said.

The two walked slowly down the dirt trail towards the boat house.

CHAPTER 56

Don't Start

"It's two in the morning, and the submarine is still there. Over," Carl said into his DNR radio.

A dispatcher on the other end acknowledged.

"Wait, I see two people walking down to the boat house. I can't make them out yet. Too dark. I'm going to check it out. Over."

"Negative, Carl. Stay put. You know your orders," ordered the dispatcher.

Carl didn't answer. He had already dropped anchor earlier and had the dinghy ready to go to shore.

"I'm going to solve this spy terror shit once and for all. I'll get that special agent position for sure this time," he muttered in a low voice as he boarded the small boat.

The rubber craft was powered by an inexpensive electric boat motor. Carl beached the little dinghy and pulled it further onto the bank. He then pulled out his pistol and proceeded to the boat house along the shore.

CHAPTER 57

Sweet Kisses in the Night

Elizabeth and Jack stopped by the two pine trees just in front of the boat house. The *Wolf* was still there on the deck of the pontoon boat. Its conning tower was still open.

"I was so scared, Jack. The fire, those people, that boat—all because of us. You went to jail," she said before totally breaking down in tears.

The two quietly looked at each other. Jack was quiet, and Elizabeth looked at him with confidence. He brushed back her hair from her eyes. In that solemn moment, they kissed again.

The night would have been absolutely perfect if it wasn't for the boating accident. Elizabeth was finally happy. She had met Jack and had started having strong feelings for him. This wonderful moment in her life helped her deal with the sadness still deep inside her from the loss of her father, an emptiness that he was buried in a cold grave and that she could never see or hold him again.

Everyone else was in the house asleep. However, tonight was Elizabeth's to hold on to and cherish. Even if it was only for a short time.

"What's going on in that head of yours?" Jack asked.

Elizabeth snuggled her head on his right shoulder and squeezed his hand.

"I'm fine. This is where I want to be."

CHAPTER 58

What's Mine Is Mine

"Mr. President. Mr. President. Sorry to disturb you, sir. You wanted to be informed when the strike team was in position to recapture the Buford Dam in Georgia," an aide's voice said softly from an intercom next to the President's bed.

"Minimal to no casualties, correct?" the President asked.

"The commanding officer of the mission said most affirmative, sir," the aide replied.

"Alright. Get things started. Have my Cabinet members meet me in the communication room. I want that commander in there as well. Also, have the Air Force reposition a low task satellite for real-time surveillance. I want no screw-ups," ordered the President.

"Oh, two more things. I'll have my breakfast during the meeting. The First Lady will have hers at the usual time. Also, I want that jackass of a governor from Georgia on the phone and ready for me to talk to him," he added.

In minutes, the White House staff was in a flutter to have everything prepared. The President used the ability to have the White House's conference room as a secondary command center. Normally he would be in *Air Force One* in a combat situation, but this was far from ordinary.

The President was about to commit an act of aggressive behavior against a fellow state that had seen war before. Not since the American Civil War had an offensive operation been called for against a rogue governor in a southern state.

The plan called for a Ranger battalion attached to the Tenth Mountain Division to conduct a water and land assault. Twelve zodiac boats known as torpedo assault boats, each equipped with high-torque electric motors, would split into two groups, forming a pincer to approach the dam by water from opposite directions.

A smaller detachment would make a *ruse de guerre* and feint an assault through the service gate and entrance.

The assault would commence at 0630 hours after a planned communique sent directly to the Guard unit's frequency. The message would be a fair warning that neither side should engage in combat and a peaceful surrender was to be expected.

There would be no charges made against the Georgia Guard troops, and their entire unit would incur no bad blemishes for these past actions. The radio transmission would be sent at 0615 hours on all bands used by the Guard unit.

Even though this upfront strategy would tip off the defenders to the impending assault, its real purpose was to go into the history books that every diplomatic chance was given to surrender peacefully.

"The men are in position, Mr. President," said an aide-de-camp.

Hart, the President's chief meteorological scientist who had warned of the approaching Hurricane Isaac a few days before, slipped a note to the Commander in Chief.

The note read: "Significant weather impact of high winds and torrential flooding in the Lanier basin may cause a catastrophic load onto the heavily burdened dam. Emergency flooding must begin at 1600 hours today and last until 0500 hours to prepare the lake to receive this weather event."

The President, after reading the note, folded it in half and stuffed it in his folder. He then nodded to Hart and thanked him for the update.

"Legal, what's the status of those Georgia boys? Are they mine to control?" asked the President.

"Mr. President, sir, with all due respect, we have been over this before in the other meetings with the Senate committee. The Georgia National Guard are classified as Title 32 troops, which means their commander in chief is Governor Nodell. You have control over Title 10 troops. Regular forces," cautioned the attorney general.

"What if I enact emergency powers and take command of the Georgia forces?" asked the President.

"That will require Congress, Mr. President, and it will take time," said the attorney.

Clearly frustrated, the President took a sip of his breakfast coffee and glanced over to Hart. The meteorologist slowly shook his head.

CHAPTER 59

Pardon Me

Elizabeth and Jack were quiet as they finished another kiss. She had stopped crying and was comforted by Jack's attention.

The comfort and peaceful bliss lasted for another minute until someone came out from behind the trees near the waterline.

"Well, well. It seems that I have the two terrorists and the illegal submarine together again. We just met a few days ago. It was you two that night sneaking up on me in Wild Man's Cove and spying on me with that camera boat," Carl said as he trained his newly acquired pistol towards the young couple.

"What? We don't know what you're talking about," answered Elizabeth sternly.

"Oh, I'm afraid you do, princess. You see, I picked up your second spy boat in the water when we arrested you. You, my dear, had the R/C controller in your lap before you dropped it," Carl said softly.

He walked closer to the couple to see them better. The moon illuminated the boat dock, but the couple was in a large shadow to the left against a tree. The other tall pine trees also cast their shadows onto the ground, adding to the limited visibility.

Carl made one more step towards the couple when a flurry of hands appeared before his face and grappled his neck. Strangely, he felt his head move sideways as he was realizing that he was under attack.

He felt an unusual snap in his neck, kind of like a bad day at a chiropractor's office. The heavy pistol fell from his hand. His body went limp as he began to feel numb all over. As he started to drop, he noticed he was still aware of everything, but he couldn't breathe or move any part of his body. When he hit the ground, the impact finished him off.

Elizabeth and Jack stood absolutely frozen in fright. First they had been held at gunpoint; now a new danger had taken charge.

Brian, dressed in total black from head to toe, didn't stop to admire his grizzly work with Carl. In one fluid move, he picked up the pistol. Before he completely brought the gun up to point, Jack made his move.

Jack leaped towards Brian and the gun.

"No, Jack!" screamed Elizabeth.

Brian was one step ahead of Jack. He came down hard with the butt of the pistol catching the back of Jack's head behind his ear.

Jack dropped to the ground, unconscious, near Carl's body.

"You killed him!" cried Elizabeth.

"No, he's just out cold, but I will kill him if you don't do what I say. Now get in the pontoon boat," he ordered.

In minutes, the boat was underway and headed to where Brian had parked the truck.

CHAPTER 60

I Gotta Go, Daddy

Her cold, wet nose touched her master's elbow. Soon a warm, fuzzy chin replaced the nose with a gentle nudge.

"What? You have to go again?" asked the owner as he climbed out of the bed grumbling.

The dog headed downstairs, knowing her master was not far behind. The owner was groggy from his three martinis and a heavy dinner. He opened the back door and didn't realize that he had forgotten a step. Finally free, she bolted.

The man, still in his bed robe, quickly realized that he didn't leash his dog and that she was running free outside.

Like he had been overdosed on super-caffeinated coffee, he ran out the back door as well. His heart pounded in his chest as fear swept through him to look for his dog.

Around the corner of the house, there she was, at the Moori's basement door. She was sitting with her paw lightly scratching the door. A light could be seen through the window.

"What's the matter, Sweetie?" asked the man as he patted her on the back and quickly attached the leash to her collar.

In the respite, the man smelled a faint odor—not terrible, just a smell like old paint left in a can and soured by rainwater. Then he instinctively looked through the window and saw Mr. Moori on the floor. He was not moving and was in an awkward position.

"Oh my God, girl. We've got to call the police. Come on," he said.

CHAPTER 61

Evil Discovered

The police unit that was the first out for the early morning shift change received the 911 call.

The address was emailed to the squad car's laptop. Data, address, who is who, and other pertinent information was pulled up on the soft, red screen. It was a color ideal for people driving in the dark who didn't want to lose their night vision.

"Hey, isn't that where that goofy guy was yesterday when we investigated that abandoned taxi cab?" asked one of the officers.

The other officer hit the lights and called in that they were responding.

Within minutes, they were across town and pulled into the Moori's drive. Both officers got out and separated. One went to the front door; the other, the rear basement door on the side.

By that time, the neighbor had come back out minus the dog who was barking in the kitchen in protest.

“Hello, officer. I'm the one who called in the report. Mr. Moori is on the floor inside. You can see him through the window," he said.

By this time, the other officer had come around from the front. He shook his head indicating that there was no activity up front.

A call on the radio requesting for backup was made. In the distance, a police siren could be heard as it answered the call. A fire truck and an EMT unit was dispatched on their way as well.

The first officer, the corporal, tapped on the window. When the body of Mr. Moori didn't move, the officer broke the glass on the basement door and reached in. Unlocking the door, the two police men entered.

"Mr. Moori? Sir?" one asked.

A hand touched the side of Moori's neck for a pulse. The body was cold. It appeared that the neck was broken from the way it was twisted.

"He's gone," the officer whispered.

By this time, the other squad car arrived. The other responders arrived a minute later.

The corporal looked around and quickly assessed that this looked like some type of a lab or illegal weapons manufacturer.

When he saw the leftover boxes of shrimp eggs, two eight-inch plastic drainage pipes, and other parts lying strewn on the floor, an old but familiar uncomfortable chill ran up his spine. Grasping his Kevlar vest around his neck like he had done in Fallujah, Iraq, the corporal was suddenly back— in country.

"This isn't right. We are in some deep shit, buddy," he said.

This was a bomb maker's basement and he knew it. Glancing around, he saw a video camera on a tripod. It was aimed at a wall bedecked with a black, religious-scrolled Arabic flag. A cushion sat in place as it was used by its owner when the videos were made.

"Central, this is 96. We need a detective here quick. We have what appears to be a terrorist's hideout. Contact command on how to proceed. We are continuing to sweep the house. Over," the corporal said into his radio.

With that, the police officer shook his head, grabbed his vest again and rotated his whole head and shoulders to shake off that old, creepy feeling.

"I thought I had left that all behind," he muttered as he walked up the stairs, his hand opening the safety snap holding his service pistol.

This was going to get ugly.

CHAPTER 62

Duty and Honor

The command post for the Georgia Guard unit was inside the 24-inch poured-concrete walls of the Buford Dam. Nestled in an office and control room, the six officers and staff huddled around their tactical radio. A makeshift antennae was rigged to the outside. They waited for any new information. There was an unusual tension that stifled the men. Ironically, in the deep, bunker-like control room, it was very cool and comfortable. The lake water at the bottom of the dam was over 158-feet deep and was at least 12 to 18 degrees colder than the lake water's surface temperature.

The massive, green-painted pipes and valves dwarfed the soldiers. There were also the three hydro-turbines that sat in an eerie silence since the dam was closed off from releasing water.

"Super Beaver, this is battalion," broke the silence within the group. The nomenclature came from the unit stopping up the dam.

Captain Bowler, a 42-year-old reservist who was extremely proud of his family's Georgia military heritage, stood up and answered the call. As the captain picked up the handset, he tilted his Kevlar helmet back. He responded in a terse voice, "That's not very funny, Williams. This is serious and you know it. We are ready to copy; what do you have? Over."

"Yes, sir. Sorry. You are ordered by the governor to disregard any communications from the regular Army or other forces. Over," Williams replied from the other end of the radio.

"This is way beyond exceeding our orders. First we were to protect the dam. Next we were ordered to arrest the engineering department and lock everything down. Now you are saying we are to ignore all military channels? This is absurd. I protest this order and want it confirmed in writing," he demanded.

The captain bit down hard on his lip and hoped the pain would override the confusion in his head. He was a soldier, but he had two commanders. Deciding which one was the right choice was the captain's demon on his back. If he made the wrong decision, his men would be killed and families would be confused—or disgraced—because they did not know the cause of this calamity.

By then, some of the men looked at him for answers. The captain's senior NCO just shook his head quietly. Things had gotten out of control.

"Captain, call coming in from a brigade commander. It's from the Tenth Mountain, sir," reported the communications tech.

"Captain, we better answer that call request," said a lieutenant.

"No, dammit. I have my orders from the Governor."

Everyone in the control room got quiet. It was 6:15 a.m. They all knew that this was their wakeup call, and they understood the seriousness of the situation since a special combat team of unknown strength from an elite Army division was going to attempt to do something.

"Click the mike three times, then three long holds, and then click three times again. And I want you to do it at least two more sets," ordered the captain.

This act was of course recognized as three dots, three dashes, then three dots. It was Morse code for SOS.

Then the captain ordered the radio operator to switch to the governor's battalion frequency and try once more time for a confirmation of the recent order.

There was no other reply.

"I'm going topside for a look around. Inform the unit to stay frosty, and no one—I repeat, no one—is to fire until I order. Is that absolutely clear?" ordered the captain.

"Sir, that's against procedures. A sniper could easily really ruin your day," said a sergeant.

The rest of the men acknowledged. The captain ignored the advice and walked out.

Outside was a stair well for both inside and outside the dam. Since the captain needed some fresh air, he chose the outside exit to get out.

Some fellow soldiers saluted the captain, and one soldier pointed towards the Buford Dam's gated entrance.

"Sir, looks like someone from Tenth Mountain wants to talk. They are waving a white flag. That will mean a parley, sir," announced one of the men who was actually a transfer from Louisiana.

The captain nodded and, with a lieutenant, proceeded to the fence. He was well aware that in a combat situation, one would not readily expose himself to enemy fire. However, this was a police action, at best. It was a mistake made by the governor. This was not a combat situation. Everyone was on the same side. All the captain wanted to do was to get out of this predicament that he and his men were in.

"Captain, I'm Major Brecker. You know my unit; you know what we are capable of doing. I've been ordered by the President to recapture this federal dam. There is a major hurricane coming this way, and we have got to open those flood gates. Now, my men have your unit in a tiny pocket. That pocket is in your hands as to your next move. We are not at war with each other. Hell, you Georgia boys showed some real guts back in Afghanistan. That combat engagement in the lowlands back during the Surge was textbook fighting. I even remember someone from Georgia giving me a great cup of coffee. The soldier said it was from a coffee company in Gainesville, Georgia. Dam good coffee, captain," the major said.

There was a pause for a moment to let his words sink in. The only sounds were from the radios from both sides making radio checks and maintenance clicks.

"If you follow Nodell's orders, there's going to be some boys hurt on both sides—some even killed. That's war. This, captain... this is not war. This is reality. Stand down. Your unit may retain their weapons. You may even march out on your own back to your base, but you and your men must leave. Those are my terms. I'm going to give you thirty minutes. Let's end this, Mark," continued Brecker as he held out a hand to shake as a gesture of peace.

The tactic worked. The captain was surprised that the major knew his first name. The captain had purposely kept that name as quiet as he could to keep himself at a distance from his men. If the major knew that much, he must be fully prepped on Captain M. Bowler.

Then, quietly, Bowler saluted the major, and then shook his hand. The occupation of the dam was over.

"The dam is yours, Major Brecker. Give me a few minutes to assemble my men. We will assemble over there in the parking lot," Bowler said.

Instantly, both sides communicated on their radios, informing their chain of commands to the change of ownership.

The two commanders and their staffs saluted each other and went back to their units.

CHAPTER 63

Mosquito Buzzing

The squad's automatic weapon was very heavy and very loud. Known as a SAW, it was an ideal weapon to fire a lot of ammo downrange to keep bad guys at bay. Built to be easily carried, the SAW was a soldier's favorite. There were two soldiers manning the SAW covering the lake approach to the dam. A few hastily made sandbags acted as cover for the two machine gunners. The large release gates were no longer visible, as the dam had exceeded its safe water level and was approaching its emergency spill-over channels.

"Are we going to have to stay here all day?" asked one of the gunners.

"Shit. The mosquitos are already out. Give me a dip," said the other.

The two pondered their position and looked to the banks and far out into the lake for any signs of trouble. Seeing nothing, they opened the can of snuff and each took a pinch to put in their lower lips. A moment to relax.

"Damn, dude. What is this stuff? I'm buzzing already," asked the soldier.

"It's called Sasquatch Bold."

CHAPTER 64

Under New Management

The empty dock he had noticed earlier at Hall Harbor gave Brian the chance to park Moori's truck close by. The parking lot allowed the transfer of the materials to the submarine. Dock J was the perfect dock for this clandestine action as neither guard house nor Marina Café could see his movements. The snails had been carefully packed by Brian in hoses. Heavy as the hoses were, he managed to drag each one to the pontoon boat.

Elizabeth was forced to help carry the other materials to the dock from the truck. She wanted to run away, but she knew the man would kill the Cotter family later at their home. She was crying and wanted to know how Jack was doing.

When the pontoon boat was fully loaded, Brian pointed his gun at Elizabeth and told her to take him to the dam. It was still dark, but the lake was illuminated by a crescent moon.

Brian tied on the six 8-inch hoses filled with the greenish snails to the Wolf's sides and on top of the lifting pontoons. The catalyst of freeze-dried shrimp eggs was in a five-gallon bucket with a locking lid. It was placed inside the submarine along with a large bag of scaegrots that Brian had fished out from one of the holding tanks. He glanced at the controls, the motor throttle, the dive valves, and even admired the periscope.

"Is that all I have to do to make the sub work?" Brian asked.

He held the pistol back to Elizabeth's head to remind her he was in control. Elizabeth pondered a moment and then pointed to a corner of the pontoon boat.

"You need those sandbags to help make the submarine dive," she added.

He pointed at the three bags. She acknowledged with a simple nod.

"You have done well. I will not kill your family. Your last job will be to lower me into the water near the dam from the boat. Then you may leave me, for I have my last *jihad* to make," he added.

Elizabeth stood silently at the helm of the pontoon boat. It was making nine knots in the still lake water. The morning sun had just started to come up; the sky turned from black to orange in minutes. Her hair flowed with the wind, hiding a tear from her eye. If she could only do something to stop this man.

The pontoon boat approached the entrance to the inlet where the dam's gates were located. It was an unimpressive cove. Huge orange floats attached to a warning cable stretched in a semicircle formed a perimeter for all boats not to approach any closer.

Elizabeth slowed the boat to a crawl then came to a stop.

A red signal flare was shot in their general direction from an outpost on the other side of the dam on top of the earthen part. The bright red phosphorous of the flare burned like the hot, red sun in the early morning twilight. The marine radio on the boat came to life on the universal emergency channel 16.

"Unidentified vessel, stop where you are. Proceed no further or we will open fire. This is the Georgia National Guard on a military operation, and you are in a danger zone. Do you copy? Over," said a soldier on the other end.

"Soldiers? Army soldiers near the dam? Excellent. My victory over these infidels will be more rewarding," Brian said as he overheard the radio transmission.

Brian's next action was to rip out the radio from its housing on the pontoon boat. When it was torn away, he threw the radio into the lake. He didn't want Elizabeth to warn anyone.

After that, Brian got into the sub, closed the conning tower, sealed the hatch, and motored off towards his target. He stayed on the surface and looked through the periscope. The *Wolf* normally travelled faster while on the surface, but it was burdened with the six heavy hoses. Brian knew that the snails would float some while in the water. It was the actual drag that slowed the submarine. He pushed the electric motor's throttle into full thrust. The light was still hazy as the *Wolf's* dark gray hull blended into the dark, still waters of the lake. Soon bubbles began to appear on both sides as Brian opened the valves and began his dive.

Elizabeth turned the pontoon boat around and began to travel back home. She reached into her pocket for her cell phone to call for help only to find that Brian somehow must have stolen it from her back pocket. Scared and feeling very alone, she tried to wave at the soldiers on the dam to warn them. Unfortunately, she was too far away to be seen individually.

She turned the wheel back around and kicked the boat into high gear and drove in circles to draw attention.

The *Wolf* had gotten away.

CHAPTER 65

Kidnapped!

"Elizabeth? Elizabeth?" the father walked throughout the house calling her name.

Michael and Steve came out of their bedrooms.

"What's wrong, Dad?" Steve asked.

"I can't find her. She's not in her room. Let's look outside. Last night she was by the swing," the father said as the three proceeded to the kitchen.

Not finding Elizabeth at the swing outside, Michael looked down towards the boathouse. He saw someone face down and another person trying to get up.

"Down there!" he shouted.

The three hurried downhill. What they found was gruesome. Some overweight, dark-haired man was on his stomach, not moving or breathing. Jack was nearby on all fours. A gash on the back of his head had dried blood as if he'd been hit and perhaps knocked out.

"Jack, are you okay?" the father asked as he knelt down to hold the boy in his arms.

Jack slowly awoke, only to have a severe headache, and he moaned for a few seconds.

"A crazy man with a beard killed that man and took his gun. I tried to protect Elizabeth and get the gun before he did. That's when I must have gotten hit. My head hurts."

"Can you stand up?" the father asked.

Slowly the two rose and headed up the hill to the car. Michael and Steve stayed behind.

"Notify the police and wait here. She might come back. Tell the authorities what happened here. Michael, get a tarp or something for the dead man. Be respectful," said the father as he helped Jack into the car. They then drove on to the hospital.

The moment their dad left, the two raced to the boat house. Steve grabbed the gas can and a funnel, and Michael untied the line on their big jet ski.

Steve, ever cautious for those wasps, looked all around the boathouse for his winged enemy. None to be found, he was thankful that he didn't have that problem to deal with right then.

"We've got to find her," rallied Michael.

Michael didn't bother to tease Steve about his fear of wasps, for it was about this time last year at Science Camp that Michael had gotten popped right between the eyes by a yellow jacket. His face had swollen shut from the bee venom so that his eyes squinted like a smiley face with its eyes shut. When Steve went to go see him, he didn't recognize his own brother.

In less than a minute, like a race car pit crew, the boys had topped off the jet ski with fuel and were on their way. The objective: find the pontoon boat, and they'd find Elizabeth.

CHAPTER 66

Look at Me!

The Tenth Mountain troops, hidden in nearby coves on their assault boats, received word that the dam incident was over. Slowly they began to emerge from their concealed positions.

Elizabeth's actions in making the pontoon boat go in circles did attract the attention of three zodiac assault craft. Within a few minutes the boats started their electric engines and approached the wayward craft.

"Tell the Major that there is a girl driving her pontoon boat in circles. We are going over to see what she's up to," radioed one of the soldiers.

"Finally someone is coming!" cried Elizabeth.

The team pulled up to the pontoon boat when Elizabeth eventually stopped the craft for the soldiers to get aboard. With weapons ready, they boarded the craft cautiously. After quickly assessing that Elizabeth was not a terrorist, the commander of the group settled down.

"Young lady, what are you doing out here all alone and driving in circles?"

Elizabeth was coming out of a state of shock when she realized that she was finally safe with the soldiers.

"That crazy guy killed a man—and maybe my boyfriend—then stole our two-man submarine." she said.

"Whoa, whoa, a submarine?" he asked.

"He is going to do something to the dam. He headed that way," Elizabeth said as she pointed towards the orange boom.

"Major, we seem to have a terror attack in progress. Request we get helo air support and for our group to engage a hostile two-man submarine.

Location, the release gates of the dam and the warning boom," radioed the commander.

CHAPTER 67

The Video

The police officer and his partner came back down the stairs, disgusted. In the basement, the medical team was wrapping up Mr. Moori in a body bag and placing him on a gurney. The detective was already working on the television and video recorder.

"Got it. Let's see what's on the tape," he said.

A few flickers on the screen and then suddenly there was Brian, dressed in traditional black robe and black head scarf. His face and beard were clearly visible. His eyes were dull and lifeless like someone possessed. He announced on the video in English that he intended to strike a blow for the lost brothers who fought the American soldier's occupation of his beloved country. He continued his rant about the new movement of ISIS that was sweeping the lands. Brian praised Allah that he had the wisdom and the gifts from Mr. Moori to use these weapons against the dam.

"Holy shit! Did he just say that he is attacking the Buford Dam at Lake Lanier?" the detective asked as he spit out the toothpick he had from his breakfast meal.

Brian, in the video, continued to say he planned to capture that submarine in the news and use it to make the attack. He continued that the weapon he would be using would continue to poison the waters of Atlanta with a red vengeance for an eternity. He finished the video with praises to Allah, his brothers in arms, and to some woman named Anya.

"Dispatch, we got some terrorist claiming he's attacking Buford Dam this morning with a submarine. We see all kind of poisonous and weird stuff here. Looks like some kind of bio bomb. Call the military, FBI, DNR, HAZMAT, Coast Guard—crap, call everybody to get to the dam quick!"

The detective was screaming into his radio by the time he finished.

CHAPTER 68

The Wolf Is Discovered

The Georgia guardsman responsible for touching base with the SAW team on the other side of the dam had a difficult time finding the right exit door to get to them. The machinegun team didn't have a radio, so they had to be told that everyone was leaving.

"Come on. Which is the right door?" he said, panting as he hauled the tactical radio on his back.

The radio crackled again as the reception was not very good inside the dam. Its massive, reinforced concrete and steel structure dampened any radio frequencies. It worked fine a few minutes before, but now it was a just a metal box on his back.

The long, narrow hallways that honeycombed the insides of the dam were used by technicians to do periodic checks on structural integrity. Most of the corridors were marked with green, rectangular signs that read a grid coordinate. The concrete walls were cool to the touch as millions of gallons of water were just on the other side.

Another metal door came into view; this one actually read "EXIT."

The moment he opened the door, he realized that he had found the correct one. The tactical radio sprang to life. The radioman was bombarded by numerous radio transmissions of a battle.

"Hostile. Hostile. Hostile. We have visual on the target submarine approaching the dam. Permission to engage hostile," the helicopter commander asked on the battalion network.

"All units, all units. You are authorized to engage the enemy sub. All units be advised, the enemy Tango is a midget submarine, position one hundred meters from the dam. Its intention is to use a bio weapon to take out Atlanta. This has been authenticated by authorities. Get that sub and its cargo!" commanded the voice on the net.

CHAPTER 69

Buzzkill

In the distance, a Blackhawk helicopter from an air support wing attached to the Tenth Mountain could be heard approaching at a high speed towards the dam.

The SAW machine gun nest that was on the lake side sprang to life. The very relaxed soldiers, who had enjoyed their smokeless tobacco break, crawled up from their slumber-like buzz to see why there was a helicopter on the lake. Dizzy and somewhat disoriented from the nicotine high, they shook their heads to wake up.

What they witnessed was several dark green zodiac boats filled with troops who had approached the dam from different directions. They also saw the helicopter as it slowed to approach the dam's cove. The lake's smooth surface was quickly chopped up by the rotor wash.

The two soldiers began to panic. They were told a terrorist threat might happen—but not an army. Especially not the United States Army attacking the dam.

"Get ready, Paul. We're in deep trouble," the SAW gunner said as he cocked the squad weapon.

"Shoot the first boat. Aw, this sucks. Do we really shoot these guys?" Paul asked.

"Hey, you two! Don't shoot! The Captain says we're pulling out!" yelled the radioman who finally got to them with the message.

.

CHAPTER 70

Splashes!

Brian began to sweat inside the *Wolf.* Through the periscope, he made out the outline of the dam's release gate. He had made good progress. The normal water currents were either still when the dam was not discharging or mildly swift towards the concrete flood gates when opened. The gray hull camouflaged the small craft well due to the lake's murky green water. Normally clear, the lake had been flooded by mud and debris since the dam hadn't had a full discharge in days.

"Almost there," he said to himself as he continued to look through the periscope.

Brian approached the orange boom that was about 20 yards away. He prepared to dive the submarine to get under the warning cable. Rolling the seat forward, he opened the water valves to submerge.

Then, with a silent pop, the periscope shattered. Brian tried to look through the lens again, but he could only see pieces of glass and lake water in the eye piece of the sub's periscope. The *Wolf* had just lost its only eye to the surface. An Army sniper from one of the zodiac assault boats had received the same "Engage Enemy" radio message.

Frustrated, Brian opened the diving valves more to make the *Wolf* go deeper to avoid any more bullets.

"He's going down, sir," observed the waist gunner over the helicopter's intercom.

The pilot called back to the gunner to see if he could engage his M60 machine gun.

"Negative, sir. The bullets would splash and possibly ricochet. Too many friendlies around. Besides, sir, the rounds would just ping off that hull," answered the waist gunner.

The pilot swung the helicopter's tail around 90 degrees for a better look. He then switched his frequency to communicate to the assault boats as well as his own crew.

"Listen up, fellas. He's going to go deep, and we'll need to change his mind or he'll be gone for good. We are engaging with stun grenades. Fragmentation grenades might damage that deadly cargo command warned us about. These grenades might not damage him with shrapnel, but we'll bust him up with the concussions underwater.

“Don’t directly hit the sub, but if he surfaces, charge in and rip off those 8-inch pipes or hoses. Seems the bio weapon is full of snails, dangerous when set free, so you'll have one chance to get this right. Here we go.

“Waist gunners, men, drop the grenades one at a time from each side. Stop when I say stop. We've got friends down there, so stay sharp," the pilot finished.

CHAPTER 71

The Wolf Is Cornered

The jet ski with Steve and Michael approached the combat zone. They could see Elizabeth and some soldiers on the pontoon boat. A green zodiac boat was tied up alongside their family boat.

Elizabeth saw the jet ski, and she noticed that her two cousins were waving frantically at her.

"That's my family over there, sir. Please, will you let them come here? They built that sub you are attacking," she asked as she pointed towards Steve and Michael for the soldier to notice.

"Hey, Hoss! Let the two boys on that jet ski at six o'clock come on through. They might know how to defeat that sub," radioed the commander.

Within a few minutes, Steve and Michael were aboard the pontoon boat and had embraced Elizabeth. It was an unusual site for Michael to see that their family pontoon boat was now a command center for the assault on his *Wolf*. Many of the soldiers on the boat acknowledged the brothers with a nod.

"Are you alright? We got worried that you were hurt. We saw the dead man. Jack's okay. Dad took him to the hospital," said Steve.

"Here, tell everybody on this radio what the weaknesses are on that sub you built," said one of the soldiers to Michael.

"Well. Its hull is heavy metal from an old propane tank. I don't think your bullets will do much damage. However, she's probably running low on her batteries. There's just so much air left inside for him to breath. The surfacing air tanks have not been recharged. He might not be able to come up. That's about it," Michael said into the mike.

The Blackhawk moved into position, hovering about 25 feet above the waterline. Everyone in the area turned their attention to the depth charge attack with the hand grenades.

Two tiny, little metal balls fell from either side of the helicopter making two small splashes. In three seconds, a burst of water shot up from where the grenades had fallen. The spray from the artificial geysers turned to a bright mist underneath the helicopter's rotor wash causing miniature rainbows as the sun's rays shone through.

Another barrage was dropped with the same result. It was soon followed by another. The explosions looked like two humpback whales broaching the surface to exchange air.

Below, Brian was in misery. He was severely tossed around inside the sub as concussion after concussion shook the little submarine. His ears bled, as the concussions had burst his eardrums. The intense pain, similar to an ice pick being stabbed into the ear, made him cry. His actions hastened his use of valuable oxygen. Every breath was a struggle. To Brian, it was like being surprised when you've walked a mile on the treadmill at 3.5 miles an hour and suddenly someone bumps the incline meter to really steep.

His head pounded as well. He knew he had to go on. His plan was still to use Moori's scheme to get close to the concrete flood gates and release the snails when the gates discharged. He looked at his watch that his father had given him when he graduated high school. He had 20 minutes to get closer.

Another series of explosions rocked the *Wolf*; this time one explosion dented the conning tower in, deforming the hatch of the sub and causing Brian's head to smack against the other side of the tower.

"That's it, skipper. We're out of grenades. We couldn't bring him up to the surface. He's barely visible now. Pretty deep looks like," radioed one of the waist gunners.

The helicopter climbed up higher to keep the rotor from washing the zodiacs around. The attack had ended in failure. Some of the combat soldiers on the zodiacs waved their brethren forward. They took turns throwing their grenades into the water. Nothing but dead fish floated to the top from the many blasts. Everyone was angry and disappointed.

Brian's eyes rolled from the last hit. He was tired and exhausted, but he had survived the Americans futile attempt to sink him. He pushed forward the dive planes and throttled the sub to full speed again to begin his last dive to the bottom. He planned that when he reached the gates, either by hitting the dam's concrete wall head on or by lucky guess, he would then allow the sub to rise to the surface. When he surfaced, he planned to open the hatch; cut the rope lines to the snail hoses, releasing the eco-weapon; and pour out the shrimp eggs from the bucket. He only had seconds before the soldiers would find him and start shooting, but he was pleased that the submarine had proven to be bulletproof. The small sack of snails inside the sub were to be used in reserve.

"I am a hero of the cause. I am an angel of death. My name will be remembered with the Martyrs. Death to the imperial infidels! Death to the United Sta—"

Brian didn't complete his tirade.

For at that split moment as he tried to say the word "States," a bolt of intense nerve signal energy reached pain receptors in his brain. It was a new type of pain—a burning pain which grew hotter by the second at the back of his ear.

Then another hit, and then another one. This time on his cheek and one on his left nostril. Brian was screaming now, and he heard a strange sound. It sounded like tiny, little wings. It was as if tiny devil fairies stabbed his face and neck with fiery, red hot pokers. He looked towards the back of the sub. In the back of the sub, Brian found the source of his pain: a broken wasp nest that had fallen into the sub sometime the night before from the boat house.

Its defenders, angry at the multiple concussions that they had had to endure, ventured out in a coordinated sortie to attack. Brian was the closest target for their vengeance.

He waved frantically inside the sub; he tried to swat down the wasps. For every wasp he crushed or swatted, another red-winged avenger took its place.

Brian leaned back to hit the nest and perhaps squash the remaining troops inside their grayish paper home. In doing so, Brian rolled backwards and his feet caught the electric throttle causing the boat to slow.

With his body weight now to the rear, he didn't realize that the *Wolf* had changed its trim. It began to rise to the surface rapidly.

Another wasp strike had popped him on his forehead. This strike totally blinded him with venom and pain as his eyes closed shut.

With no downward propulsion, the *Wolf* pointed upward like a dead goldfish in a water tank. She rose and breached the surface. The sub's bow and the damaged conning tower protruded out of the water. The *Wolf*'s sigil was barely visible.

From the pontoon boat, Michael, Steve, and Elizabeth witnessed the broaching and saw their sub with its stern deep underwater. It looked like an abandoned water bottle floating on the top. The *Wolf* was helpless.

"Young lady, did that man have any weapons or bombs that you know of?" asked the zodiac commander.

"He had a pistol, a bag filled with sea shells, and a pickle bucket," Elizabeth said.

"Remember, everyone, the black plastic pipes are filled with some sort of biological weapon using snails. Don't let him release them. Also, new information is that he's armed with a pistol," radioed the boat commander.

"What's a pickle bucket?" asked another soldier.

"I'm sorry. I worked at a hamburger shop, and the pickles came in those green five-gallon things. The lid is very hard to unsnap. It's built that way to keep liquids from spilling out. What's odd, though, was that he didn't have the crow handle." she explained.

"I'm sorry. Crow what?" asked the boat commander.

"The tool to pry open the twelve clamps on the bucket," she answered.

A short distance away, a small battle took place. Army zodiac boats, each with an assault team of four men, quickly approached the sub. As each of the rubber boats crossed the orange float boom, the outboard motor was raised so that the turning prop was clear of the wire cable. Once clear, the boats moved quickly and connected to the *Wolf*. The soldiers, armed with their combat knives, cut away the snail-loaded hoses from the hull. All six were cut away and carefully stowed on board one of the assault craft. One of the hoses had been damaged by the concussion grenade attack and a large group of the snails spilled into the water.

A soldier removed his Kevlar helmet and scooped up the some of the still-floating snails before they had a chance to sink. His fellow comrades all did the same and prevented other snails from escaping. The helmets were then carefully put onboard the zodiac boats.

At this point, the sub was like a sardine can that had no pull tab to open it up. The men tried to open the conning tower, but the wing nuts were on the inside of the sub. This prohibited any entry to get to the terrorist inside.

"We can't get in, and he's armed with a pistol. Blow it," shouted a commander.

Three soldiers attached demolition explosives: one to a diving pontoon; one to a corner of the conning tower; and the last one to the prop and rudder in the rear.

"Get clear. Fire in the hole! Fire in the hole!" shouted one of the demolition experts as he pulled the fuse ring to activate one of the timers.

The other soldiers did the same. They then re-boarded their assault boats and quickly sped away.

Designed to blow off locks and door hinges, the explosives would do the job of disabling the submarine from any other action.

CHAPTER 72

Losing Her

Brian could only hear the soldiers climbing around on the outside of the hull. The *Wolf* bobbled like a large cork with the additional weight of the men onboard.

His face was full of whelps from the many attacks from the wasps. The swelling on his forehead made his face and eyes tighten and hurt.

Then he heard the sounds of the motor boats going away.

Three explosions rocked the *Wolf*. The starboard side flotation pontoon was blown off. The hull was blasted, but there was no penetration, no breach. The third explosion was underneath the rear of the *Wolf* near the prop and the two oxygen tanks that were used to bring the sub to the surface. The blast was meant to break away the air tank, but it had no effect.

Brian's equilibrium was shaken beyond repair. He suffered miserably from the wasp stings, ear drum bleeding, head concussions, and so little air left. Now with these three additional explosions, he was a horrible wretch.

Unbeknownst to Brian, one of the blasts had broken the positive clamp on one of three marine batteries. This wire had come loose from the terminal but still touched it randomly. This powered the lights and the sub's electric motor. They would flicker on and off intermittently, further adding to Brian's misery.

"She's sinking," said one of the soldiers on the pontoon boat.

Elizabeth, Michael, and Steve walked to the front guard rail of the pontoon boat to get a better look. Someone handed Michael a pair of binoculars.

The *Wolf* bubbled all around its waterline as the sub slowly slipped beneath the water. She died as the vital oxygen of the air tanks used to keep her afloat bled away from the damage.

"There she goes," whispered Michael as he held the binoculars.

Steve had put a hand on his brother's shoulder, and Elizabeth leaned in to show her support and sense of loss. In a matter of seconds, the *Wolf* was gone.

CHAPTER 73

The Death of the Wolf

Brian was vaguely aware that the submarine was going down for the last time. The lights inside the sub blinked off and then on randomly, which startled Brian each time.

"I must not fail," he gasped with each word.

The *Wolf* flipped to its right side which threw everything, including Brian, practically upside down. The sub began a downward spiral towards the lake's bottom. The bag of scaegrots had spilled open, and the snails, still safe inside their self-contained shells, were tumbled and tossed throughout the inside of the sub. The spill sounded like a bag of seashells being dropped onto the floor.

The bottom of the lake was at least 158 feet down, close to a sixteen-story building in length downwards. Pitch black and extremely cold, the lake's watery depths embraced the *Wolf* as she plummeted deeper and deeper. The sub's metal hull moaned and popped under the strain. The conning tower's bolts holding the hatch closed made the most noise as they stressed under the immense building of pressure.

Brian tried to turn around. When he did, his foot finally kicked the battery wire free. The electric arc from the battery shot through his ankle and leg towards his groin, causing immense pain. A rancid smell of burnt flesh and cloth filled the cabin. He knew he was never going to see light again, for there was no way to get that wire back on the battery terminal.

He reached blindly for the five-gallon bucket that was filled with the freeze-dried shrimp eggs, the catalyst to activate the scaegrots. He finally touched the lid of the bucket and grasped the handle.

Brian tried to pull the bucket towards him, but he was upside down and pinned against equipment in the sub which had broken free from their placements. He continued to pull, but it wouldn't budge. His fingers started to bleed as the plastic clamps on the lid cut into his hand. He had hoped to expose the snails to the shrimp egg feast when the waters eventually rushed in. He knew he could still cause havoc if the snails could get water and eat. They could reproduce and do their worst. He prayed for the hull to break open under the strain, but it never did.

Then there was a large jolt. Everything inside shifted with a sudden jerk as the *Wolf* reached the sticky, muddy bottom.

Brian couldn't cry anymore; there were no more tears. He could no longer take a full breath, just shallow sips of air. In total darkness, alone, marooned on the lake floor, he passed in and out of consciousness. There were only a couple of minutes left before there would be no more breathable air.

Brian then started to hear something from the snails. The sound was like the muffled popping of popcorn in a microwave. Their mucus plugs had dried out causing the inhabitants' instant death. The released methane from the deceased smelled horrible to Brian and added additional misery.

Brian knew he had to hurry to save the rest of the snail rout. With one hand trapped beneath him and the other barely able to move, he tried one last reach to twist a wing nut to one of the bolts holding down the conning tower hatch. If he could get the lake water to rush in, he knew that the other bolts would fail in succession and that the sub would flood. The snails would get their water and live.

He made one half-twist of the nut and tried for a second twist with twelve more rotations to go, but then he heard a noise that finally put fear into him that this was his end.

It was that familiar sound of wax-paper-like wings which fluttered near his face. A couple of wasps had escaped from their destroyed nest. One wasp, not able to see in the pitch black darkness, bounced off the inside of the sub's wall. He landed on Brian's shoulder and started crawling towards his neck.

A lone air bubble left the confines of the sub's last remaining air tank and started its long journey to the surface. It traveled along the underside of the dead sub. It dribbled up the side of the hull, past the conning tower, past the *Wolf's* stenciled image, and then finally upward towards the surface. If one were that bubble, one could have heard Brian's last dying word.

"No!"

CHAPTER 74

Sadly Coming Home

"Let's move on, men. Our job is done here," ordered the leader of the assault boats over the tactical radio frequency.

Michael took the helm of their boat and paused to look at the spot where the *Wolf* had gone down. The assault team did a GPS location of where the sub went down and then sped away to meet up with the rest of their unit.

A few minutes passed, and Elizabeth and Steve both wanted to go home.

"I'm so tired and hungry, guys," she said.

"Yeah, Michael. Those clouds are getting dark and it's misting. Looks like a big storm, so let's go home, okay?" added Steve.

Reluctantly, Michael slowly turned the boat around and headed back. Steve jumped off the pontoon boat, started up the jet ski, and followed.

The rest of the Tenth Mountain troops made their way back to the dam in zodiacs. Transport trucks were routed to a boat ramp to load up the watercraft and men.

The Georgia guardsmen began assembling in the parking lot. The control room was reconnected to the central control station located in Columbus, Georgia.

A radio message was flashed to the general of the division. It confirmed the sub kill. The scaegrot-filled hoses were contained with minimal impact to the lake. There was no evidence of breakup debris floating to the top, so the submarine should probably still be intact.

A special dive team, with specialized underwater gear, was needed to reach the wreck 158 feet down. A heavy-lifting crane was also needed to remove the submarine from its watery grave.

CHAPTER 75

Celebrations

"You have your victory, Mr. President," praised a general in the executive staff room.

"We still have that hurricane barreling down on North Georgia starting tomorrow, sir. The dam must get relief as soon as possible," cautioned Hart.

"Good. Alright. Get me through to the Corps of Engineers. I want those floodgates opened to ease the stress on the dam, and I want it going within the hour," he ordered.

"It has already been done, sir. Also, the military states that there are no traces of any snails or other biological wastes coming up from the wreck. Looks like our boys got it all," said an aide.

Hart smiled in approval and gave a thumbs-up to the President.

Other staff members hurried to alert other officers, sections, and—more importantly—the media.

Since the news broke about a submarine sinking a recreational house boat, possible terrorists, and rumors of a military take-over at the Buford Dam, multiple news agencies had set up camp to catch the latest story. A press conference was scheduled to comment on the tense actions that day.

CHAPTER 76

I Have an Announcement

At the Georgia capitol building in downtown Atlanta, the members of both houses were summoned for an emergency announcement.

Flanked by two Georgia State Patrol officers, Governor Nodell approached the podium and adjusted the microphone. Camera crews and journalists waited for the important announcement. The immense chamber room grew quiet.

Telia sensed the chamber's mood and held her hand to her earpiece and nodded to the cameraman to start.

"We're breaking live to bring you this exclusive story of the governor's announcement that he has been successful in concluding the debate over the water usage. Yours truly has read a copy of his speech, and I can honestly tell you it was a very impressive feat that our governor has accomplished. Let's listen," she bragged.

"Ladies and gentlemen, my esteemed colleagues of both the Senate and the House, distinguished guests, and members of the media, it is my distinct honor to inform you that the water usage dispute over Lake Sydney Lanier is officially over. In my hand is an official memo that the state's attorney general has acquired. It is a signed agreement that allows Atlanta to continue to use the lake and allocates that bordering lakes, such as Lake Harding and Lake Seminole, share their resources to be added to the mighty Chattahoochee River.

"All three states agree that this is not—and I want to be clear—not a federal issue for some federal arbitration judge to decide over. Outsiders from the North do not know how we live. They are not familiar with our customs or our histories. They do understand our very Southern fabric or even how we tick," he said.

Nodell was interrupted by both houses as they gave a thunderous applause of approval.

"It is therefore imperative that we mend our fences with our neighbors and also be good stewards of all water resources."

Again there was another interruption of applause. That time, everyone stood while they clapped.

An adjutant placed an index sized note on the podium for the governor to read quickly during the second applause.

It was left on the lectern and simply read: "Dam recaptured by elements from the Tenth Mountain Division. Our troops have surrendered. Treaty is being revoked by Alabama and Florida state attorneys. Legal repercussions and sanctions will follow. The President wants you to fly to Washington to meet with a special oversight committee on your actions as a state governor and probable removal."

The governor's face grew ashen. The applause had died down by then. Everyone returned to their seats and waited for more of this great speech. The media personnel had seen a note handed to the governor, making them extremely curious as to its contents. They noticed he had dread in his eyes and face and that his hands had begun to quiver. The press smelled blood.

Telia, with her microphone, listened quietly as she thumbed through the pages for the next part of the speech. She didn't like when politicians went off script.

The governor went silent. He started to mumble something. He couldn't form any words. Total paralysis overwhelmed him. He could barely breathe. His left arm started to ache. His heart pounded. Tremendous droplets of sweat poured down his face, chest, and back. His right hand went to his chest, and he clutched it tightly. He looked up to the ceiling, blinded temporarily by the bright lights of the chamber, as if he longed perhaps for Heaven, but then his eyes rolled to the back of his head and he collapsed.

He fell to the floor, his left hand still grasping the state attorney's memo that the treaty was signed and the deal was done. A great victory for Georgia was to be his legacy for generations to come.

Like a mighty Georgia pine tree being cut down by a lumberjack, his body made that same heavy, dull thud on the podium floor. Governor J.C. Nodell died, and then his left hand released his most cherished memo.

CHAPTER 77

A Fresh Start

Mr. Cotter waited by the boathouse as the pontoon boat and jet ski pulled into the slips.

He ran onto the dock and hugged the teenagers, crying tears of joy. All four embraced in happiness as the rain started to fall.

"Where's Jack?" Elizabeth asked.

"Oh, he'll be fine. I talked to his dad and the authorities. My lawyer helped plea the case down. We'll share the cost of replacing the burned-out houseboat. Jack will be under house arrest until the whole thing settles, but he can have visitors," the father said with a wink to Elizabeth.

She smiled and hugged her uncle a little tighter.

"I also heard from your mom. She'll be home tonight. She's upset about you guys using up her good scrap iron and her best equipment, but she'll get over it."

"Why's that, Dad?" Steve asked.

The father held the kids tighter and pointed with his right hand that was around Michael's neck.

"Because a surprise just drove up to keep Mom happy," he said.

At that moment, Mr. Maney honked his truck horn as he sat in his big rig. The rig had pulled a huge trailer into the driveway. It was filled with many large pieces of scrap iron, welding supplies, and everything else a sculptor needed.

Michael and Steve quickly started to smile because of what they saw next. As the family walked up the hill and turned the corner of the house, there it sat. Alone, strapped to the back of the trailer, there was another silver-painted residential propane tank. It too had been cut open for safety reasons. Purchased as scrap from an old house that was being demolished, the previous owner's name was written with a can of black spray paint. It read: Wolf.

Thank you for reading my book. Please visit my website for news, photos, and information about the forthcoming release of the two other books with Michael and Steve Cotter.
Please visit: edthilenius.com

ABOUT THE AUTHOR

The son of a television sportscaster and a loving mother, Ed Thilenius grew up in a world filled with imagination, religion, and adventure. These three factors opened up his mind to not only create fascinating stories and characters, but to engage the reader (or player) in his world. With a degree in History and Geography from West Georgia College, Thilenius has authored many versions of many historical battles and designed numerous award-winning board games.

His first novel, *Wolf on the Lake*, is the first book in a trilogy focusing on the Cotter brothers and their adventures. This novel has already begun a debate among friends and family about homeland security and protecting our natural resources from terrorism.

Thilenius is currently working on his second book and is promoting his current work as a guest lecturer.